THE VEIL OF SNOWS

THE VEIL
OF SNOWS

Mark Helprin

Illustrated by
Chris Van Allsburg

VIKING • ARIEL

For Alexandra & Olivia
M. H.

VIKING
Published by the Penguin Group
Penguin Putnam Inc., 375 Hudson Street, New York, New York 10014, U.S.A.
Penguin Books Ltd, 27 Wrights Lane, London W8 5TZ, England
Penguin Books Australia Ltd, Ringwood, Victoria, Australia
Penguin Books Canada Ltd, 10 Alcorn Avenue, Toronto, Ontario, Canada M4V 3B2
Penguin Books (N.Z.) Ltd, 182-190 Wairau Road, Auckland 10, New Zealand

Penguin Books Ltd, Registered Offices: Harmondsworth, Middlesex, England

First published in 1997 by Viking, a member of Penguin Putnam Inc.

1 3 5 7 9 10 8 6 4 2

LIBRARY OF CONGRESS CATALOGING-IN-PUBLICATION DATA
Helprin, Mark.
The veil of snows / by Mark Helprin ; illustrated by Chris Van Allsburg.
p. cm.
Sequel to : A city in winter.
ISBN 0-670-87491-4 (alk. paper)
I. Van Allsburg, Chris. II. Title.
PS3558.E4775V45 1997
813'.54—dc21 96-40040 CIP

Printed in Italy
Set in Stempel Garamond

LIST OF ILLUSTRATIONS ·

IN MY ROOM, ON A SHELF, IS A BLUE BOTTLE OF GLASS so dense and uncorrupted that to look at it or through it is to enter a sapphire, there to be held without breath or desire as if in a world stopped still. It is filled to the top with water from the stream that runs through the village. If you turn it upside down, no bubbles rise. If you peer through the cobalt blue glass you see no indication that the bottle holds a liquid. In fact, did I not know what was in it and were it not so heavy, I would assume that it was empty.

I have had the blue bottle for twenty-five years. The water in the mountains is the best in the kingdom, as prized in the far-off cities even now, in a time of corruption, as it was in a time of purity.

1

Though I treasure this bottle, the day will come when I drink from it and toss it from my wooden balcony, grateful as it shatters on the rocks below, for on that day all the water that runs through the kingdom will be pure and full of promise, and as life resumes with all its possibilities I will have no need for relics. But until the waiting is done I'll bide my time, as I have been biding it up to now.

I'm hardly content, but I have no choice other than to wait. I chose this place because of the high view it has of the march-lands and the Veil of Snows. Every day I see in the distance sunlit cornices and banks of ice, and bright mists that race across fields of light in pursuit of blinding sunshine. In the saddlebags of the horse I led down from the mountain, I found the bottle that has become the one remaining object of the old kingdom, the symbol of my hopes and the vanishing point for my devotion.

Many a day has passed when I have forgotten what I am waiting for, and failed to watch the confusing play of light and shadow in the Veil of Snows. Sometimes, I may forget for more than a day. Has it been as long as a week? I think so. Or perhaps several weeks, or a month. Time passes here in its own way, but whether very slow or very fast, it takes you in upon its worlds upon worlds.

And there you always find something, a bright contrast, a

2

surprise that wakes you up, that gives strength and renews faith, even if only because it reminds you of what you've lost and how much you still love. It happened again this morning, when I went to fill a bucket with the water that, charged with the life of the kingdom, will someday overflow with the vitality of the present. The stream was running so full that I had to go to a different place to draw the water, down the street of stone walls to a windblown pool. Just below this is a weir that foams the stream until it's white with its own velocity and strength.

I'm not young. I was tired from carrying the empty bucket, and dreaded carrying it back full, especially up the stairs, so I sat upon a bench that with the rising of the stream was now so close to the rapid that I felt as if I were riding on the back of a swan swirling on the tide. I breathed the fresh air that rose from the agitated current and let my head fall back until my eyes were filled with perfectly blue sky resting upon the pointed rooftops of gabled wooden houses. As I stared past the fronts of yellowing varnish and boxes of blood-red geraniums I was thinking neither of the queen I loved, nor of the Veil of Snows, nor of her son who vanished there. I was merely old and tired, and passing time in the sun. I don't remember how long this lasted, but after the shadows rose and fell and I felt rested, I picked up the bucket and knelt by the edge of the river. I dipped the bucket in and pulled out what seemed to be just air and sun as white as snow, and as the white water settled into the clear, I watched half of what I had drawn out simply disappear.

As I was thinking about this I looked down at the stream, and there running swiftly past me on top of the foam were clotted chains of scarlet and crimson, tangling, sinking, diluting, and disappearing. My bucket fell into the torrent, never to be seen again, and I staggered back, electrified by memories of a different time.

The crimson and scarlet lines were not the blood of men, women, and horses, but merely dye that a laundress had loosed for an instant upon the stream. As fast as it had appeared, it was gone, perhaps chasing the lost bucket, and the water was white so soon afterward that I wondered if I had imagined this, especially when I looked up to see that the laundress I had glimpsed was no longer there.

Having come to fetch water, there I was without a bucket, next to a river speeding by in immense volumes of foam and spray carried upon cold black currents in obsidian gleams. And there I was, an old man in the sun, about to begin the difficult walk home, up thirsty hills and thirsty steps, to a house in which the only water that awaited me was in the blue bottle.

✢ ✢ ✢

THOUGH ONCE I WAS A SINGER OF TALES, THEY WERE not very good, for I always put too much of my heart in them, and never enough (I was told) of calculation. Where others would captivate and entertain, I would only sing a simple song that bent its head as if in prayer before time and truth and love. It was all I could do, and all I wanted to do, and I don't know why. I followed nature's wild rivers and God's glittering lights, and they led me into a land where I was alone.

I was neither afraid of my solitude nor unhappy about it, but, lacking an audience, I could no longer be a singer of tales, and I became what I am now, which is I don't exactly know what. Perhaps I am a kind of sentinel. My little house is high on a hillside overlooking the village, and from only mediocre height it has a commanding view of the great march-lands and the Veil of Snows. But though a sentinel, I do not merely watch. I wait, and I have formed an image of exactly what it is I hope to see.

Long ago, in the time of the old emperor, I was young and just beginning in my profession. The usurper was there, and one could not escape his evil presence. With his inexhaustible schemes, numerous agents, and terrific powers he often seemed about to prevail, but the old emperor, who had been through many more battles than he, always held him in check. That there was a struggle between what was, in the main, good, and what was, in the main, evil, and that time after time the good prevailed, made all the children born in my time believe that this was the natural order of things, that even if it took a great deal of effort, effort would always find its reward and the just would triumph, as would the innocent.

I still believe, which is why I am on a hillside waiting. And I certainly believed then, even as the usurper began to gain the upper hand. Surely, I thought, the crimes that bring him power will soon bring him down. Waiting then, as now, I did not change my songs, as did the other singers who listened carefully to everything that was new, and soon I found that I was nowhere, they were everywhere, and the usurper had taken the throne.

Can you imagine my surprise the day that he sent for me? Why would he bother with a singer of the old songs? Why would he bother with me? But he did bother. He cared inordinately, as if his life depended on it, as if I were his most vexing opponent. This I could hardly believe, and not only was I flattered, I was so afraid that my heels shook as if in an earthquake. As soon as he began to speak, however, I realized that I need not have feared. Either he would kill me, and I would have eternal peace, or I would beat him with courage alone. Were he not actually three times my size, he

certainly appeared to be, and this was multiplied by his rank and disdain.

"You are still singing tales in the old style?" he asked, his voice as sharp as the point of a lance and as deep as the beat of a drum.

"Yes."

"Where?"

"Well," I said, "times have been rather tough. I sang by a merchant's campfire not so long ago. A caravan was taking empty lard cans to the nether outskirts of Zilna."

"How many?"

"How many lard cans?"

"No, idiot! How many merchants?"

"One."

"You said a merchants' campfire."

"Yes, a merchant, and his campfire."

"You sang to one person? Isn't that demeaning?"

"I've had worse."

"You've had audiences of less than one?"

"My career has had its ups and downs. It is possible to sing to no one, and lately I've been doing that quite a lot."

As if remembering his own difficult times, the usurper nodded. For my part I prayed that I would not begin to like him, although I cared very little if he liked me or not, for I knew that even were he extremely fond of me he could have me dispatched as easily as cracking a pumpkin seed. He had passions, and he sometimes killed for them, but he killed most often and most vigorously out of calculation, for to him all of life was a battle, and the object of the battle was to conquer all.

"Why is it then, that my agents call you a threat?"

I suppose he wanted me to write my own dismissive obituary before he killed me, but, in defiance, I would not. "They tell you, Emperor, that I am a threat, because I am a threat."

"Singing to a single merchant about to journey a thousand miles with a bunch of empty lard cans?"

"Even had I sung just to the cans themselves."

"And how is that?"

"As long as I sing, a song is there. And if a song is there, someone might hear it and sing it to someone else, who would in turn sing it to someone else, and so on and so forth, until eventually it might become the anthem of the armies that will send you to oblivion."

"Then I shall have you killed."

"I was not expecting otherwise, and it hardly matters. My songs, though not very popular, will remain. The Damavand sing them even now. And someday their horsemen, riding at the head of the armies, will have cause to sing indeed. You are using actualities to fight potentialities, and that, Emperor, is a worse nightmare than any you can visit upon me."

"We'll see," he said, in a voice so deep that the chalices shook.

I was expecting to die right then and there, but he said, "I order you to unravel your singing."

"I beg your pardon?"

"Unravel it!"

"Meaning, sir?"

"Your songs," he said, impatiently. "Un*do* them."

"I can't. They're already sung."

"Then sing them again, differently. Sing them so that they are about me. Sing them so that when people hear them they will weep for my sacrifices and admire my powers."

At this I laughed, which must have astonished him, knowing as he did what he had in mind for me. "I would not laugh if I were you," he warned.

"Why not laugh?" I asked. "I know how you will torture me, but I know that I will not sing the songs as you would have me sing them. You might as well try to burn water, because I'm water, and water doesn't burn."

I then spent the next years of my life—the longest years I

remember—in the deepest torture chambers underneath the loftiest prisons. By some chance or interference I refused to die, day after day, until finally the armies of the young queen captured the city and freed us all. No longer a singer, and fit only to be a soldier, I joined the victorious armies just as most everyone else was leaving them. Of low rank, broken memories, and no prospects, I knew nonetheless that a new struggle was inevitable.

IT WAS A SUMMER VICTORY, I WAS FREED IN AUGUST, and I passed into the ranks on a cold and rainy day in September, the first day of a season that can be either bleak or clear. The induction hall was cheerful as soldiers mustered out, moving into the newly liberated civilian world. The place itself had been an army watch station, of which the old emperor had built a hundred, and the usurper a further nine hundred. They were all of stone and heavy timber, with vast spaces, and fireplaces so gargantuan that in one of them half a dozen cooks were working amid just as many tables and three or four separate blazes, all under a single mantel.

"This is one of the usurper's former watch stations," said the sergeant in charge, really a baker I had run into from time to time before the revolt. He was a strange man, small and fat, as furry as a baby bear, with two enormous and blazingly white front teeth. His name was Notorincus, and though his bearing was entirely unmilitary, he was a capable soldier.

"How do you know it wasn't built by the old emperor?" I asked.

"The torture chambers underneath."

"Ah yes. The torture chambers," I replied, with no evident emotion.

"And also, these barracks, which have not been enlarged, hold a hundred men. The old emperor's watch stations held fifty. All he needed throughout the city were five thousand soldiers, and they had nothing to do. With a hundred men at a thousand stations, the usurper had a hundred thousand, and they never rested."

Notorincus saw that I glanced repeatedly at the cooks. "Are you hungry?" he asked.

"I'm very hungry."

"That's no reason to join the army."

"Of course. My hunger and my enlistment are coincidental."

"Still," he said, almost brushing me away, as bureaucrats do when they imagine that in signaling a person out of the room by making sweeping motions over their desk they are doing God's will, "why don't you eat and then come back, to see if you really want to join. I'll account it as a recruitment expense."

I agreed. The cooks at the nearest fireplace were stirring something in a huge cauldron. "What's in here?" I asked, and the answer was provided by a woman in Balarian cap and gown.

"First," she said, "we roast venison, wild turkey, boar, and pheasant, continually drenching them in a marinade of red wine and fresh herbs. Then we slice the meat and throw it into the cauldron. We add pure water carted here from the mountains, and as this cooks we prepare the vegetables. We roast potatoes, parboil carrots and celery, and braise half a dozen wild lettuces, armandellos, and spoots that have flavors both strong and subtle.

"All is added together to boil and simmer for many hours. It is a royal recipe that the queen has made the army's own. You may have some, but don't eat too much. You cannot be fat in the army." She looked at Notorincus, seemed embarrassed, looked at me who was still starved, and cast her eyes down.

As I am not the kind of person who would join the army for a meal, I returned to Notorincus after I had eaten, and he took down my history and questioned me about my fall. "Why didn't you simply alter your songs?" he asked, gazing at my scars, of which there are so many that even to this day I can be only a man alone.

"I couldn't."

"Why?"

"They had already been sung. They existed."

"But why not change them as requested?"

This question puzzled me. "Never was there the possibility that I would do that."

"Why?" Notorincus pressed.

"I suppose it's because they're like people," I said. "They may be like dumb or ugly people, or people who are deformed, but I couldn't just take their names, annihilate them, and issue new ones, could I?"

"I suppose not, if you think they're like people, but are they really?"

"Yes," I answered, nodding. "They have in them something, sometimes a great deal, of the people I love, some of whom are lost forever. Therefore, I could not have split them like wood, or carved them like stone. It would have been a betrayal, and it would have corrupted the world."

"The whole world?"

"Just my part of it," I said, "but that is, after all, the part for which I am responsible."

"You would have died rather than abandon the old songs?"

"Yes."

"But life is so precious."

"Yes."

"It is paramount."

"No."

"No? Then what is?"

"Love," I said, "and honor."

"Excellent!" said Notorincus. "Excellent! I'm sending you directly to the Queen's Own Guard, my regiment. You don't look very good, but we'll get you back on your feet and train you until you are master of horse, sword, and bow. I myself came to the ranks knowing virtually nothing, and now I'm nothing but a soldier."

"You were a baker, weren't you?"

"You knew me?"

"I remember your stand at the night skating."

"I can still bake, I haven't forgotten. It's like riding a bicycle. Sometimes a brioche or a Sacher torte appears in our barracks," he said, "quite mysteriously."

"I see."

"And you? Can you still sing tales? The queen loves the singing of tales."

"No," I answered. "I cannot. I have in me only one more tale, and I must wait to see it before I can sing it."

✦   ✦   ✦

SOON AFTER I HAD BEEN TRAINED, I WAS BROUGHT to the queen. Service first as a conscript in the old emperor's army and then as a reservist had made horse, sword, and bow part of my nature, but I did require a year to regain my health and strength. A little more than a year, actually, and Notorincus escorted me to the royal apartments in October, when the mountains were gold and the air was bright.

Though the queen could have had a hundred fires burning and never had to tend a one, she kept a small blaze in a modest terra cotta stove the size of an orange crate, and this she took care of herself, with evident pleasure, feeding in new wood and stirring the coals with a plain wrought-iron poker. I don't imagine that the usurper has ever touched such a thing, as even the handles of his heaviest swords and most horrible maces are filled in white gold.

I was surprised by the modesty of the royal quarters. Though some of her tables were of spectacular intarsia and the oldest, darkest, most glowing woods in the world, others were of pine and quite rough. A huge painting of the battle of Valò made one wall a world of color, but on another a long peg rack held swords and bows, quivers of arrows, coils of rope, military clothes, and leather saddlebags filled with bedding, food, and tools. The queen, who had since childhood been a soldier and who took nothing for granted, including her station, was to be proved horribly right.

But at that time the victory had just been won, adversaries pardoned, prisoners released, soldiers returned, and she could freely show all the beauty of her youth and triumph. I confined my emotions to loyalty. As one of the queen's common subjects, a soldier in her guard, and a much older man, I was not free to fall in love with her, so I did not. She had taken a husband in any case, I was of no rank, and, after my time in the cells, women looked away from me.

The queen did not, and her loveliness of soul, directness, her grace, and her high qualities washed over me with such delightfulness, shock, and strength that I was awakened and renewed. She was only eighteen or twenty, and her long hair, which in her youth had been golden, had in its dark chestnut color no hint whatsoever of brittleness or fatigue. Her face had no sign of flagging energy, self-indulgence, or defeat, as do the faces, if you look closely, of even many twenty-year-olds.

Hers was the kind of beauty that does not proclaim, but listens. Hers was the beauty of gentleness and trust, of devotion. She was dressed in gray, with a scarlet and gold medallion below her left shoulder, and, wonder of wonders for a royal, who is not expected to show any kind of weakness, she wore spectacles. Thin tortoise shell, the same rich brown color as her hair, they held lenses of such clear crystal that the transparency generated touches of gleaming silver.

This was our queen, whom I loved the moment I looked upon her, for whom I would sacrifice, for whom I would die, and whom I would obey. Once I had seen her from a distance, upon a balcony, and that was enough to make me twice loyal. But in her presence my life changed, as did my purpose, which is what royalty are for, though mostly they strive and fail to imitate those few, like the queen, who give to the word *royal* its meaning and good name.

I sank to one knee and bowed as I was required both by custom and my own heart, and, by God, all in surprise, she took a sword and knighted me. I, a broken man, a good soldier, a failed singer—a knight!

"Rise!" she commanded. And, as I stood, I looked into her face.

"Madam," I said, my voice choked with emotion. "I don't understand."

"Do not feel that you have been chosen without merit or in damaging haste. I took command of the armies as a child, a girl. I was not a man, and could not make my decisions as a man. I was not old, and could not make them from experience. And because the fate of all rested upon them, I learned to draw from depths that

21

others were not forced to find. I learned to act with the speed of a hawk tucking in its wing for a dive. Perhaps I might have been more deliberate, but the opportunity was not there, and I for the rest of my life must do things the way salmon jump, waves roll, and trees bend."

Notorincus, who had remained, smiled, because he had been with her in victory after victory, and when she had risen from defeat.

"At the battle of Lichtengaard, over which I presided when still a child—it was the first major battle of my life—one of the soldiers in the ranks was singing a song of yours, only one soldier, and I took from it a line that I have carried in my heart ever since, for not only did it serve me that day, but when I say it even now I feel love and truth as if they are waves that are lifting me from the ground."

I did not ask what line it was, and she did not tell in this, my first meeting with her, and though I was in her guard and frequently saw her from afar, some years would pass before the next.

 AGAIN SHE CALLED FOR ME IN THE FALL, BUT THIS time in November, when gray skies rolled with dark woolly clouds, and the fire in the terra cotta stove was

bigger and brighter. She seemed much more a woman now, though not too much time had passed, and of course I went down on one knee and all that, but though I was thrilled to see her I didn't smile or glow the way people do in the presence of royalty. I wasn't there to have my buttons polished but to serve queen and country. And this she knew, which is why she called for me.

"The father of my child," she said, holding her baby up in the air and moving him to and fro until he smiled with the game, "has seen him only once. All this time, he has been at the head of the armies, in the march-lands, with the Damavand. My husband is used to living in the open, used to moving under the weight of armor and sword, used to cutting the flow of streams with the passage of his war horses, used to directing men with nothing in their eyes but the cold blue sky. And yet, when he came to his son, he held him with tenderness such as I have never seen, he rocked him, and kissed him, and tears fell from his eyes onto his polished armor.

"Soldiers fear that their children will be left without them in a cruel and pitiless world, that they will not be able to pass on to them the skills of self-preservation. My husband said, 'The boy and I must ride together so that I may teach him to be the match of any enemy. Already I am plotting to make him a master of horse, this infant, this tiny baby, whom I must leave so soon,

23

though I hope not forever.' That is what he said, and then he had to leave.

"As queen, it is my duty to ensure that mothers may teach daughters, and fathers may ride with their sons, for from the beginning of time these have been among the best of things that some seek to overthrow."

"Who?" I asked.

"Who? Those who cannot abide by simple beauties and things of the heart. Those who chafe at unreformed tranquility. Those who would tear parent from child for the sake of ambition or idea." She went to the window, and I followed. When she walked she moved as smoothly as a swan gliding through water.

"Look over the streets," she commanded, and I did, easily, for although her apartments were modest they had a stunning view. The city was spread below us as if we were standing on a cloud. "There you can see a hunting party coming in after a day in the fields. Soaked by squalls and buffeted by the wind, their oilskins are glistening, their eyes bright, cheeks red, and noses cold. Their bags are filled with stiff and bloody birds, their limbs are sore, and their hearts contented. Tonight they will eat and drink, and then sleep deep sleep by the fire, with dreams of primal things, of arrows flying, blue skies scalloped with black cloud, of death and the rain."

"And yet these are only hunters. They pass through unguarded gates and troop through the city in peace, but when I hear the hoofbeats of their horses I think of battle. In quiet times I think of nothing but that."

"You were raised in battle."

"Yes. I've done my best to learn the peace, but cannot."

"As long as the sword is sheathed until it is needed, you have committed no sin."

"Ah," she said, no longer reflective, but with fervor, "that's not what the Duke of Tookisheim says! Oh no! He, his mouthpieces, newspapers, broadsheets, and criers, say quite the opposite. They say that to be prepared is a danger to the peace, and that the implements and skills of war must be abolished."

"And what of the usurper? What if he is spit from the Veil of Snows, an army behind him and a week's march from our gates?"

"As *The Tookisheim Post* said only yesterday," the queen said, placing her spectacles upon the bridge of her nose, and then letting them slide down a bit before she read, "'such an event is highly unlikely, hardly imaginable, next to impossible. The last time a pretender returned from the Veil of Snows was in the time of the old emperor's tenth grandfather. Indeed, the last time anyone is reliably reported to have come from the mists was a full year ago, when a man dressed as a shepherd suddenly appeared on the

27

snowfield above Mannisbreim, utterly confused and from no one knows where. Why is it, then, that our resources are wasted in keeping the prince and his substantial armies at the margins of the kingdom, guarding against nothing more than a figment of the queen's disturbed imagination?'" She slowly removed her spectacles, and looked up at me in gorgeous agitation.

"In the ranks, Majesty," I said, "soldiers ask why you have not exiled, executed, or imprisoned the Tookisheims, although they know the answer, and are just expressing hope."

"Of course they know. I cannot exile, execute, or imprison a man solely on account of his opinion, which is what the usurper did. We are confident that in the wars of opinion, our views will prevail, and, if not, then not."

"Even if the fields are tilted? Nay, vertical?"

The queen cocked her head in anger. "I do not understand why every newspaper in the land, every broadsheet and every crier, is owned by the Duke of Tookisheim, or Peanut the idiot son, or, now, after the return migrations of the usurper's Damavand colonists, by other dreadful, vulgar, cheap, and grasping Tookisheims.

"I lose count. Let me see. Branco Tookisheim, from Bulgatia, makes the talking boxes that take the place of books. My statisticians tell me that he is now the richest man in the kingdom, richer even than his uncle, and much admired as a seer, although he sees nothing. How could he see anything in those diminutive little boxes full of stupid shifting colors that, when all is said and done, add up to nought?

"Bulgis Tookisheim, Branco's always unctuous brother, has corrupted the schools of the kingdom beyond imagining. I have no authority in this question, never having attended school, but in my visits I have seen that the classes are devoted to absolutely everything but study. All is games, costumes, tricks, machines, travel, politics, superstition, and entertainment."

"I know, Majesty. I was graduated from these schools before Bulgis Tookisheim made them into madhouses and penny arcades. I grieve for the students, who are obliged to float through hurricanes of idiocy."

The queen raised her left arm to a level just above her shoulder, opened her hand, let it drop, and said, with animation and despair, "The kingdom is judged anew with each generation. If its children are corrupted and distracted, the kingdom will fall. I believed after the victory that our satisfaction and relaxation would be of short duration, that memory would serve to keep us on an even keel, that having been through suffering and danger we would from the day of our freedom be responsible and true. But no. The same parties that want to disband the armies also want to punish the vanquished, who will rise against us so much the faster if they know we are weak. What is it in these people that makes them turn the wheel to which they are pinned until their heads hang once again under their heels?

"We, who should be temperate, magnanimous, hard-working, strong, well armed, and kind, are instead flighty, vindictive, lazy, weak, disarmed, and cruel. The cities are full of the casualties of love overthrown, children abandoned, and vows broken. Our diminished armies exist in the splendor of the open air, disciplined and true, but at home they are denounced. If this kingdom were not my own, I would look upon it with disdain, distrust it in alliance, and believe others in their grievances against it. I know well what will come of this. As in the blink of an eye, comfort will become peril. Suddenly, all of us—the weak, the vain, the honest, and the iron-willed—shall know nothing but war and death. How can I prevent this? I am the queen. I have powers, and it is my duty to set things right. You, who know a thousand tales, draw from them, reach back, and say what I might do."

We stood in silence, looking over the city as squalls of rain and fronts of cloud swept from district to district, now lightening, now darkening, but always moving. The lake was ruffled in blue and gray, whitecaps visible as a gloss half gone the moment it was perceived. Evening was approaching, and lines of smoke rose from countless fires that gave the air the scent of cedar and pine. I said nothing, for what I might have said would have been far worse than staying silent, and when the queen saw this, her heart seemed to break, for she was the queen, and it was her duty to see into the vales of sorrow.

As things had worsened from month to month and year to year, celebrations and distractions had become more common. When the kingdom had been moving forward with all good speed and great things were done every day, no one celebrated, for the celebration was in the doing, and our hearts were full. But when nothing seemed to work, and even the river seemed to flow only in fits and starts, the air was never clear, and the streets were never clean, the world exploded in dinner parties, ceremonies, awards, commemorations, banquets, feasts, contests, meetings, all the meaningless gleanings that were the realm of the perpetually busy Tookisheims.

The Tookisheims. The Duke, Peanut, Branco, Bulgis, Rand from Aramonia, Marco, Firco, Jocko, Bruno, Fippo, and Blottis from the Herring Flats, Malitia and Sucritan Tookisheim who ran the circuses, Rolf who made dresses, Ipwog from so far away that no one knew whence he had come, and Minty and Wissy and Patricia and Minka Tookisheim, females of the clan who had married advantageously and outlived four husbands who all had died coincidentally on the same day, of plum poisoning. And then there was little Walnut Tookisheim, Peanut's brat, who went about in a cart drawn by eight poor children, and Beanslaw Tookisheim, the electricity magnate, who made his fortune by harnessing dynamos to house-size wheels in which ten thousand chipmunks fed on meal laced with anxiety drugs would desperately try to flee overhead horns blasting out *The 1812 Overture*.

They were all over the place—not the chipmunks, whom boys trapped and sold to Beanslaw Tookisheim's agents for a derma apiece (because, needless to say, the chipmunks on the wheel had no time for courtship, marriage, and reproduction), but Tookisheims, that is; Tookisheims, Tookisheims, all around, and not a one could think. It was impossible to turn one's head without catching sight of something that had to do with a Tookisheim. Born with neither reticence nor sorrow, they charged forward from their first day to the last, convincing themselves with the progress of their success that they were worthy and good, when all the time they were hardly human and made the world so miserable that if it had been a dog it would have begged to be put to sleep.

Even the queen could not remain wholly without their orbit, and one night she went into their midst, in the time when the lights had begun to go out all across the kingdom. I was on the ramparts, guarding in bright moonlight as the queen attended a dinner honoring Peanut Tookisheim's induction into the hall of fame of the Savarins of Tropical Nuts. Peanut, you see, was a moron who, although he ran all the newspapers in the land, could not write an article that anyone could understand. They all went something like this: "Morbopus, when, after which and in which specifically it was that it did not, much less to say if then it would not, then, certainly, that which it did but with which it cannot and absolutely has to have did." His father had to establish the Savarins of Tropical Nuts so that Peanut, who was able to tell one nut from another, could collect some ribbons and sashes, which were de rigueur for any Tookisheim.

The queen had been blackmailed into attending the dinner when the Duke of Tookisheim hinted to her that if she did not he would strop the news until the ragpickers went into rebellion and with senseless and febrile abandon dived off the parapets by the hundreds or thousands.

So she steeled herself and went. As a soldier of the close guard, I stood immediately outside the dining room, on the rampart of one of the Duke of Tookisheim's pieds-à-terre embedded in the wall in one of the fashionable districts on the lake. The moon was shining in bright silver, cascading across the waters in an oxygenless beam, and were it not for the pure imbibition of its

33

cold light I would have been seasickened by the conversation from the banquet, of which I heard every word.

Though they hated her, the Tookisheims were absolutely tickled to be in the presence of the queen, and they gushed, burped, bloated, and moaned like infatuated hippopotamuses, as the poor queen could hardly stay afloat in the torrents, lakes, and sinkholes of Tookisheim vanity and inanity.

One is supposed neither to speak first nor to argue in the presence of the queen, but before she had even sat down, Rand and Blottis were going hot and heavy—screaming, gesticulating, standing and then being pushed back into their chairs by their footmen—about which was the more challenging game, ring toss or quoits. Were it not for the carefully observed commandment against inter-Tookisheim fratricide they probably would have duelled that night, struggling home after twenty minutes of swordplay with hundreds of pulled muscles and not a single cut.

"Aren't the two games almost exactly alike?" the queen asked, amazed.

"Oh no, Majesty," Rand and Blottis said, as if twinned. "They're much different! That's because, that's because, that's because. . . ." And there they froze, and were to remain frozen, mouths open, eyes staring vacantly ahead, for the rest of the dinner. On account of the splendid acoustics of the vaulted stone

ceiling, I heard the queen say quietly to herself, "Two down."

I was just beginning to smell the quick-grilled miniature Dolomitian salmon (which are filleted and marinated after being kept without food for a week in fresh spring water). Half a fish, sans head and tail and flavored with oil and herbs, is thrown for an instant on a white-hot grill, flipped like a live fish rising momentarily from the mirrored surface of a lake, and then charred on the other side. Not only do they sizzle, but the Duke of Tookisheim served them without limit, and to cool the palate he provided an argon sherbet.

"What is that, exactly?" I heard the queen ask.

"A gas, Majesty. My chefs purify it from the air. They run after it with butterfly nets and collect it in platinum flagons. Then it's chilled with a hazelnut-clotted-cream-raspberry puree. A dash of cherry brandy, and . . . *voilà*."

"I didn't think," said the queen, "that even the imperial kitchens in the time of the usurper, when they were stoked into activity as white hot as the grills for Dolomitian salmon, produced such rarities."

The Tookisheims had strained to the limits of human discipline not to mention the usurper in front of the queen, only to have the queen bring him up herself. They did not know what to say. Although they had feared the usurper as much as they had profited from serving him, they had come to profit more in the freedom of the restoration, and although they generally preferred to his dictatorship their own peculiar form of government, known among scholars as an idiocracy, they wanted him to return nonetheless because they needed his wafer-thin moral pretenses, his baroque lies, his insatiable desire for the foppish, the vacant, the fashionable and cruel—in short, for the essence of Tookisheimness. (Once, Blottis had manufactured a perfume that he called *Mooplah—The Essence of Tookisheim*.)

"Majesty," said Peanut, in a moment of candid idiocy, "we are keeping the usurper's traditions alive."

Though the other Tookisheims froze, the queen did not. "Yes, Peanut," she said. "I know. And half the kingdom, transfixed by Branco's little boxes, shares your hope for his return."

Trying to be diplomatic, the duke broke in. "Majesty, Branco sells ten thousand of his boxes each day."

"And the boxes," Branco added with pride and hysteria, "are nothing! What matters," he continued, holding out his left index finger and twisting it in the air as if he were impaling an invisible Lilliputian, "is the cards that go inside. I sell a box for fifty derma, but the box costs me forty-five derma to produce. I sell a card for fifteen derma, that has cost me one derma to produce. And for every box, I sell a dozen cards a year. Do you know how many derma pour in each hour? I need one of my boxes and a set of cards to calculate it. And what's so wonderful about all this is that I don't even have to do any work. Various idiots make up the cards, other idiots put them in nice packages, and other idiots sell them. It's like a factory. It is a factory. A money factory! I have so many derma I don't even know what to do with them. I can't explain it, but I love being rich, and the richer I get, the richer I want to be!"

"It was like that, I'm told," the queen said plaintively, "in the time of the cloth merchants."

"But that was only cloth, and these are boxes with colors!" Branco shouted.

"That was only cloth," the queen repeated, "that fell from a woman's shoulder and flowed with her as she danced, that swaddled a newborn, that kept the hunter warm as snow choked the air. Just cloth. . . .

"Whereas," she went on, having gotten used to writing decrees all day, "you, Branco, with your ugly little boxes and cards, have taken the stream of life, the wind, the cold, the oxygen, and the air, and made them a game. Branco, I have known sweat and blood, the scent of the woods, the smell of a fire, ice breaking up on a lake, the cold, the dark, the August sun, real kisses, true love, loyalty, suffering, and sacrifice. But Branco, I hate, I hate, I truly hate . . . games. And you, Branco Tookisheim," she said, her lovely eyes burning through him like a hot brand, "are turning the life of my kingdom into knock hockey."

"But Majesty," said Peanut, smiling weakly, "Branco's boxes do all kinds of things. They count the number of peanuts at the peanut exchange. They keep track of the moisture content in millions of hazelnuts. They monitor cashews!"

"How extraordinary," said the queen, so disdainfully that some of the candles were snuffed out. But then the next course was served—medallions of smoked wild turkey with truffled artichoke puree—and in the rich silence each Tookisheim stewed, wondering what disaster would be next, for it was after all a sad thing that this whole race of men, these idiots and fops, could only offend and anger the queen. My heart was heavy, for I knew how unhappy she was that all our triumphs were turning to brittle glass, so resolutely, so fast. That evening, nothing anyone might have said would have charmed her. Her husband, unaccounted for unusually long, weeks past the customary point, was encamped near the Veil of Snows, and though she longed to be with him, the capital and its governance required her presence. Her infant son, whom she held most of the day as she wrote decrees and sat in councils, was alone in his crib while she dined with idiots dressed like Spanish grandees in lace, wigs, and fly's-eyed-green satin that clasped their undisciplined bellies like luxury coverlets knit for pregnant watermelons.

These Tookisheims, I thought, and was just about to fulminate in a sentry's eye-darkening finger-pointing diatribe, when I heard a faint sound from over the wall. Though it hardly registered, it was real enough to choke my resentful monologue, and a good thing too, for never was there an angry song worth the singing. Was the sound that of a bird passing by the battlements, ghostlike against the stars? The sky was empty. Another sentry, trying to signal? I looked to left and right: all was well. Something from inside? No, it had risen on the wind.

I went to the parapet and looked over the dizzying sides of moonlit stone. The sound of waves far below combined with the hiss of air in the teeth of the battlements. Only a thin scallop of rock lay between the base of the wall and the lake, dark and wet from the hooking of whitecaps. The sole way to get there was by boat. I heard the sound again. It was a cry. And then I saw movement far beneath me. I called the sergeant of the guard, and instructed him to bring ropes, and although it took some time, he did.

I suppose I ruined that dinner by trooping my soldiers through the dining room under huge coils of rope. The Duke of Tookisheim came out, about to burst with screams he could not release because of the presence of the queen, and tried to slash me with his gaze. But his gaze was not very sharp, and what did I care? His newspapers had never published any of my songs in the days when newspapers had things in them other than articles about artichokes, and now my time of singing tales was over and I was a soldier of the queen.

"What are you doing with these twines?" he asked.

"Twines?"

"Yes. Strings."

"Ropes, you mean, or lines?"

"Lines, twines, I don't care, you're dragging them through the dinner of the century! We're celebrating Peanut's induction as a . . . oh, never mind. The queen is here, you can't do this!"

As he twitted, I was grateful to be lowered over the parapet at the end of the rope, where I found myself alone in the moonlight next to the elemental rock of a face so sheer that it was visited only by sun, wind, and snow. How graceful it is in such lonely places, how tranquil to sink slowly into the abyss, awake and alive.

Halfway down, the waves began to sound like a storm, and I could see a figure lying prone on the rock below. As I was nearing the ground I began to feel the cold spray of fresh water from the shrapnel of the waves. My right foot touched the ground in absolute silence, as if I weighed an ounce, and I felt like an angel. The lake, like a sea, was rolling, broken with white, and freezing

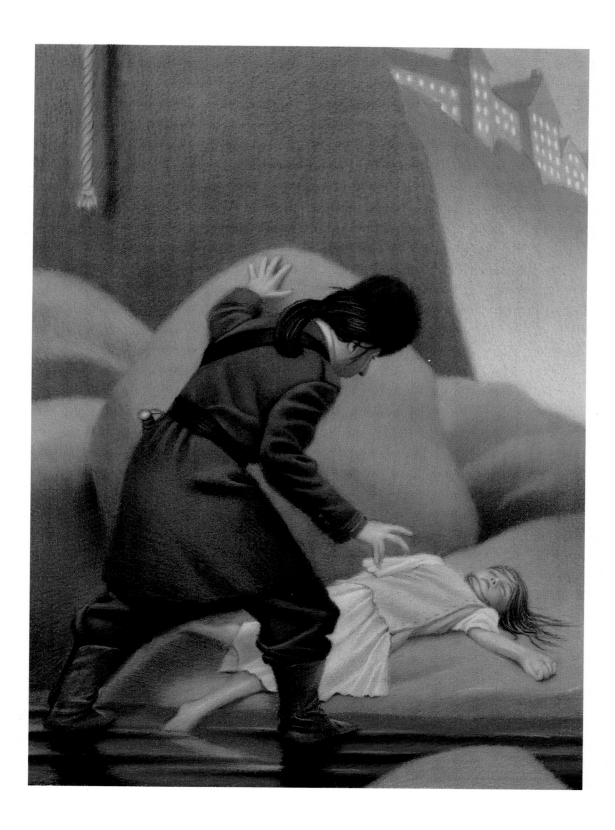

cold, and immediately before me was a child, a girl of about eight, in homespun cotton encrusted with ice. On the rocks nearby, splintered and broken, were the remains of a crude round boat called a rowell, used by the fishermen in the swamps southeast of the lake, off the narrow bay that stretches for many a day's travel to meet the inrush of the river Darya.

As I removed my coat and wrapped her in it, she hardly moved. Not expecting her to speak, I began to tie a harness into the rope, intending to loop it around her tiny waist and chest so that she could ride up with me, but as I was doing this she jumped back.

Nothing I could say reassured her, and every time I took a step in her direction she herself stepped back, until she was standing dangerously close to the water. Then I fell back a little, and she moved toward me the same distance. With no idea what to do, I sent up a note describing the situation and requesting some food with which, perhaps, to gain her trust.

When the rope came down toward us, I thought it had a huge basket tied to it, and then I thought this was a soldier. How stupid, I thought, to send a man down when a basket or a sack would do. But it was neither a basket, nor a sack, nor a soldier, it was the queen.

I smiled to think how she must have stunned the

Tookisheims, doing what they would only pay someone to do, someone whose life they thought damnable and disposable. And so it was with many kinds of satisfaction that I sank to my knees and made a deep bow, as is required when the queen comes into one's presence, even if one has been standing on the rampart all evening listening to her speak.

Whereas I had been tied securely, she had simply stepped into a loop in the rope. I was not surprised. Royal beings make their own safety and have their own style of grace. The minute she alighted she rushed to the child and warmed her with her arms, and the child, knowing the embrace that protected her was that of the sovereign, did not object. But, still, she would not speak.

"A long time ago," the queen told her, "I arrived in this city in much the same way you have, with perhaps the same fears and the same foreboding, but I learned not to be afraid, I grew, my heart strengthened, and I even became a queen. In the very first days, I trusted myself to a rope that lifted me to a high place where I had never been. Now you must trust me to take you up. It shouldn't be that hard. I was alone then, but you are not."

She put her foot into the loop, bent slightly, and took the child up, thanks to my hard-working infantrymen, as smoothly as two birds on a column of wind slipping past the sun-baked granite of a summer cliff. Soon after, I followed.

The Tookisheims, those idiot Tookisheims, just sat at the table looking on disapprovingly as the child quivered from exhaustion and cold. "She needs a bed until the doctor comes," the queen announced.

"These are business premises," the Duke of Tookisheim said archly. "We have no beds. There is no place here for dirty children from the street." He thought this well said, and a slight smile raised the corners of his mouth, near the artificial birthmarks.

"You're saying that there is no place for this child to lie down, no food for her at a table overladen with food?"

"Majesty," the duke said, his tone offensively instructional, "royalty should avoid proximity to the wretched and lowborn."

"She needs something to eat," the queen said, almost in tears.

The Duke of Tookisheim mistook this for weakness, the first unraveling, perhaps, of her authority. "Not this food," he said, "not here."

Our queen, though judicious and true and always restrained in the use of her great power, was not absolutely perfect. She was, thank God, a creature of passion, who sometimes abandoned all she knew and all she had learned for the sake of a simple thing that spoke directly to her heart.

When she extended her lithe and powerful arm, and swept everything off the table, it was, I suppose, the beginning of the

47

end. Like shot from a cannon, the crystal, the goblets, the silver, the chalices, the stemware, the dishes, the plates, and the salvers rocketed from the linen and smashed against the wall.

How wonderful to see such a beautiful queen so livid and enlivened. "You!" she commanded, in a voice that was irresistibly powerful and yet lovely and feminine at the same time—a perfect alto. "You Tookisheims! For you I now invoke the charter of national defense and declare a state of emergency. Until further notice you are impressed into my military service, with the rank, each and every one of you, of garbage handler."

"I'm a brigadier-general in the reserve!" Bulgis protested.

"You were a brigadier-general, Bulgis, and until you find work in the military garbage brigade you and the other Tookisheims will attend to this child. Her blankets shall be the finest of your damasks, her bed the great table, her food the food you were about to eat."

"Like hell!" shouted Branco, stepping back a pace, his eyes on the queen and flashing in anger. This was the beginning of rebellion, or would have been, for the instant he began to draw his sword against the queen herself, I drew mine. And by the time his sword was ready to straighten after its weak opening arc, I had killed him. Quickly following upon that, our men drew their weapons, and the Tookisheims sank to their knees and bowed, though not out of reverence.

"Arrest them," the queen said. "We'll have to let them go, but arrest them now, bring the child food and bedding, and hurry the doctor."

She turned to me. "Are we back in the days of struggle?" she asked. "Is this how it begins?"

"I don't know, Majesty," I answered, "but this is how it feels, isn't it?"

"Yes," she said. "This is how it feels."

TRYING TO COAX THE CHILD TO SPEAK WAS EXCEED-ingly difficult, for she simply refused. As I was the one who had found her, I was always asked to be present when the wise men of court tried to snake from her indelible muteness a sound that would gain them glory or position, perhaps an embassy in a place even more remote than the wilds from which Ipwog Tookisheim had sprung with many servants, shining silver bottles, catfish-leather suitcases, and frilly embroidered shirts.

Why did they think that the sprinkling of fetid waters or the burning of rare dried moss would—any more than rubbing her hand on special royal pigs or dressing her in saffron cloth—make her identify what had driven her forth? And, as in the preparations for a ball, when love of tartan, satin, pearls, and patent leather overcomes the modest, the sensible, and the true, all the wise men of court suddenly became detectives.

They cast her footprints, cooked cloth from her dress, examined her like physicians, and declared that microscopic lines in her teeth meant that her diet included a particular kind of hard and tiny seed grown only in a certain region of the Balkash steppes, where the horsemen wore round and pointy hats and all children past the age of three had a tiny golden lion tattooed upon the wrist. That she had no such adornment proved, they said, that she was the child of outcasts or rebels, or perhaps of royal blood. But others said, no, it was because her skin was unable to take the golden ink, a condition they dubbed royal golden ink dermal rejectivist floptitis. But none of this made her speak, and meanwhile messengers were sent, and couriers, and scouts, to the prince and his armies near the Veil of Snows. But not a single one of them returned, and when nothing is heard from thousands of men in a dangerous place, everyone wonders.

The queen, however, remained confident. She had seen her husband swallowed by the mist, which had then receded and shown him still standing, as if nothing had happened. "Do you know how certain of my subjects," she asked, "run off the highest cliffs with dart-like kites, and float without fear? In that way, he takes the movement of the Veil of Snows. Its blinding edges do not impress him, and he has crossed swords in oblivion with the Golden Horde."

Still, no word arrived, and the messengers, couriers, and scouts all failed to return. Nothing seemed amiss except everything. The girl in the battered rowell was the only one who had come from beyond the city in many a month, and she was paralyzed with fear. Then, one day, after watching a nitwit philosopher show her pictures of the constellations in hope of reading the mystery in her eyes, I called for Bulgis Tookisheim.

"Sir," he said insolently when brought into my presence. "Is it the state of emergency that roused me from my bed?" Of all the Tookisheims, Bulgis was the most pompous.

"Your grace graced his bed in the afternoon?" I asked.

"Tookisheims are of noble blood, and sleep without pandering to the light."

"Bulgis," I said quietly, but firmly, "if you don't want to see your noble blood escape from your melonlike body, you will go to one of your warehouses and bring me a painting of the usurper."

"I have no such thing," he said, coyly.

"You have hundreds of such things. They aren't illegal, just outmoded. Bring me one. I'm requisitioning it."

"Do you want him as a scholar? Healer? Man of science? Philosopher? Explorer? Poet? Musician?"

"I want him," I interrupted, "as a killer of innocents."

"We don't have that, of course."

"It is what he would call a warrior."

"On horseback, or standing with sword?"

"Either one will do."

Bulgis disappeared quite suddenly and was back just as fast. His warehouses and depositories were everywhere, even around the corner. A nauseating oil painting of the usurper dressed for battle was brought into the room where the philosopher was still hectoring the patient child with astronomical patterns. Even though she was headed in our direction across a sea of marble, I did not wait for the queen's judgment, for I knew she would be too kind.

Two solid and compassionate varlets set the portrait in front of the child, and she turned her head to look. As the hectoring philosopher watched unmoved, she held herself stock still for a moment that proved to be the last instant of the old era. Then she screamed, doubled over, and sobbed, as everything she had held in

52

came rushing out. I lifted her into my arms. "The usurper has returned from beyond the Veil of Snows," I said, though I did not have to say it. "And even now as we sit here doing nothing, he is conquering and killing."

EVERY MAN, WOMAN, AND CHILD IN EVERY CITY, village, and remote outpost, knew that if a single one of them resisted, the usurper would kill them all. Such immense back pressure created a paralyzing reluctance to move in one's own defense. Because the usurper wanted the village councils to be terrified and aggrieved, he would often kill even those who surrendered. He wanted someone in every village to stand and say, "If we throw ourselves down hard enough at his feet, perhaps he will spare us."

"How shall we defend ourselves?" the queen asked, as her infant slept on her lap, his tiny mouth half open, his soft limbs and little hands splayed relaxedly across the golden cloths in which he was wrapped.

"Madam, you yourself led the armies in one brilliant stroke after another to defeat the usurper. I am just a singer of tales and a common soldier, who, at the time of your victories, was chained to the wall in the Bukonsky Prison."

"I was a girl," she said, "burning with the spirit of God to conquer or defend. All was by instinct and inspiration, and nothing was to lose. Seeing this, my generals followed close on, and we had behind us the energy and anger of a kingdom oppressed for generations.

"But now the generals are old, the people have no grievance, and I have him," she said, smiling upon the beautiful child. "He has softened my heart and made me vulnerable to fear. If I am afraid for him, I cannot make the unflinching decisions that lead to victory."

"But you must."

She smiled. "I can't."

"But why me, Majesty?"

"Why you? This is why." She held up a yellowing manuscript that I had not seen in many years. "The usurper had it here, among his things," she said. "It is your tale of the siege of Vashtan Tseloe. Never have I seen tactics as brilliant, a battle more illuminating, or a fight more real. And it came from you."

"Madam, it was just a tale. I haven't commanded anything more than a company of your guard."

The queen replied, "Every battle is a story written by its victor. The skills of a general and a teller of tales are much the same:

56

how to judge a man's character, and where to put him in the line; what to strengthen, and what to neglect; how to cross a field of many paths; how to impress a skeptical enemy and lead followers who want to believe; how to judge the terrain, know the weather, and use the light; how to marshall all the many details for want of which a battle can be lost; and, above all, how to move an army forward like a song. I trust you to defend the city, and you must not let it fall."

"But why not Astrahn? No general is greater than Astrahn!"

"I've sent Astrahn with three armies to hold Bulgatia. If Bulgatia falls, not even Astrahn could defend the capital. The other generals are good at what they do, but have neither the freshness nor the imagination to defend a city that, like ours, is nearly indefensible.

"If my husband returns with his armies all will be well. Until that time, use what we have here. Find a way," she said, "to save this child, and the kingdom that someday will be his." She held her baby in the air, and, truly, he looked like an angel.

For a moment I stood still, trying to marshall my strength. I could not refuse my sovereign's order, and would not. For, in truth, I loved her, as did we all, but unlike most others I had the delight of looking closely upon her face and into her eyes. This feeling, like that of a young man in love, I attributed then to her royal grace and my unflagging loyalty, for I was so much older, and love, I assumed, was no longer open to me.

We heard a commotion in the reception rooms that led to her chamber. What this could be we did not know, for ordinarily no one dared disturb her. But then Notorincus rushed in, breathlessly, after just the pretense of a knock. The queen's eyes narrowed in anger.

"Oh your majesty," he said, "a messenger has come from the Veil of Snows. He says he will say nothing to anyone except you."

I saw the queen straighten into almost a military bearing. Her mouth quivered slightly, and she breathed deeply to calm herself. "Bring him in," she said, and as Notorincus left to get the messenger, a knight whom she had known from many battles, she glanced out the window at a kingdom that was still hers. She smiled the saddest smile I have ever seen.

In the colors of the prince's army—black armor with red sash, but now stained with blood and soil—the knight limped in, back straight, visage dark and stormy.

"Report," she ordered, as of old, but with the child in her arms.

He went down on bended knee, bowed, and straightened. "Majesty," he said. "Four months it took me to make the transit

58

from the Veil of Snows. The usurper and his multitudes have sealed the land. They rest upon it like locusts. I was captured twice, and I escaped twice. I rode on the stray horses of the dead, and in empty boats on rivers of blood. The situation in Bulgatia—"

"What of my husband, and the armies?" the queen interrupted.

"Do you not know?" the knight asked in surprise and pity.

"No," she answered, gently. "Tell me."

He then spoke what may have been the harshest words of his life. "Madam," he said, "your husband is dead, long ago, and the armies defeated. Most were killed, a few are prisoners, and perhaps some, like me, are still in the fight, but all is lost."

The queen closed her eyes and held the child tightly to her, and tears rolled down her cheeks.

"At the head of an army so vast that it blotted out the snow-fields, the usurper burst from the Veil of Snows like a sudden storm. First to ride out against him was the prince. They fought as the Veil of Snows swept close, as it had done before, but this time the usurper had grown in power. It was as if he were very much larger, as if, wherever he had been, he had found stunning and inexplicable powers. He threw the prince upon the snow and struck him with his sword.

"We couldn't see any blood, for the prince's colors are red and we were at a distance, but the mists came at great speed, the usurper stepped back, and your husband, who did not move, was taken from this world."

As the queen cried, I looked out upon the city I was charged to defend, and though it lay under a tranquil blue sky in warm afternoon light, I saw before me a picture of grief and longing. How innocent and sad are beautiful things that are about to fall.

WITH NO EXPECTATION OF VICTORY I SET ABOUT nonetheless to defend, driven by duty, defiance, and the love of queen and country. The city was, indeed, almost indefensible. On low ground that sloped to the lake, its back to the water, of immense size but long and thin as it stretched along the shore, dependent for food and materiel upon a hinterland that our weakened armies were no longer large enough to protect, it cried to be abandoned. We might have made a much better fight in the mountains, from village to village, from defile to defile.

But here were the royal palace, the ancient streets and parks, the great squares, the fountains, Ferris wheels, museums, and commercial districts that are the heart of a kingdom, even if its people are hypnotized and enervated by color boxes and do not frequent such places anymore. Let us say that their souls are not dead, just sleeping, and that someday they will awaken to the beauty and grace of what is tranquil and Godly.

I had no time to reflect as I planned the defense. We could only guess when the assault would come, but were sure the usurper was saving us for last. Then the capital would be besieged by terrified armies of slaves fighting as slaves for the principle of slavery, and all in the currency of fear. Our estimate that we had three or four months in which to fortify was right, and had we not that much time to prepare, the city would have collapsed as soon as the enemy army darkened the plain.

The queen spoke to the assembled populace in a voice that carried miraculously high and far. When the usurper speaks to the people he uses megaphones, horns, and repeaters (little fat-men who stand on boxes and instantly relay his words down long lines of frightened citizens). And his words themselves are the work of a team that spends a month destroying the simplicity of a fifteen-minute speech. His phrases leave him like shot falling upon the crowd. When the queen spoke, however, she would just stand and speak, and her easily flowing words—wise, sagacious, and chaste—left her like doves thrown to fly.

What she said was very simple. Though the enemy was quite terrifying, death itself, she was reconciled and calm, and would defy him until the very last. Anyone who chose self-preservation by exiting the city would be allowed to do so, but after five days, when the work of defiance had begun, those who went over to the other side would be executed. Bulgatia was holding, and messengers had been sent to Dolomitia-Swift to beg the help of this just kingdom whose armies had never known defeat. "I myself will not leave," she said. "With my son, who someday will be king, I will either perish or prevail in your midst."

Though a few trickled out the gates, it was best to be rid of them, for those that remained were solid and true. Then I gathered soldiers, engineers, physicians, politicians, and provisioners, and we started on the design. Our first problem was water. Even had we built cisterns the snowfall would not have been enough to sustain us: we had to continue drawing from the lake. The difficulty was that the inlet pipes were far from land and beyond cannon shot. As they were not so deep that our divers had been unable to build them, they were not so deep that the usurper's divers could not seal them shut. For this we had a remedy, an Archimedean hammer that would send explosive pressure through water, an incompressible medium, to pop any cap like a champagne cork. But after one or two tries this might easily destroy the entire conduit. We hadn't the time and it was the wrong season in which to build new inlets.

So we built a reservoir in the palace square, with walls of marine oak and every gap caulked including the spaces between the cobbles. The bulkheads were almost as high as a man, and the area flooded so vast that in it we could keep enough water to last for two years. To keep the water aerated and fresh, fifty windmills turned waterwheels that each lifted a score of immense troughs, emptying into chutes that combed the water into white foam. These did not work when the wind blew feebly, but in a squall the reservoir boiled as forcibly as sugar.

The cross walls that divided it into many lakes were not to strengthen it (for there is no more pressure on a wall holding back a given height of water if the water is as extensive as the ocean or just a hand's breadth across) but to stop wind-driven waves that with a silken rolling resonance might very well have smashed the timbers and flooded every lower floor in the city.

Our second problem was food. The old emperor had built storage structures and granaries sufficient to feed the city for five years (and the mice for five thousand). We would lack only dairy products, fresh vegetables, and fruit. To remedy this I called in the architects. "I want to know," I said, "exactly how much weight the flat portions of the palace and state roofs can hold." They reported after their surveys that the roofs were built to hold the weight of fifty consecutive snows, for construction of the palace had begun in the time of the great and unending winters, when the sun was maroon and the snow never ceased.

We hauled soil in carts and sacks, and on the rooftops we built a garden so vast you could not see the end of it in any direction. Dairy herds and flocks of sheep and goats dotted the squares of turf and brown soil. A region of orchards, carried up tree by tree, made a reddened overture to the golden autumn, but it was so far away from the queen's tower, whence I saw it, that it looked like a sparkle of sunlight.

Although I made a suggestion or two, I left to the quartermasters the task of producing the maximum number possible of cannonballs, crossbow bolts, arrows, and catapults. One especially giant machine was constructed to hurl the city's accumulated garbage onto the enemy camp. If their siege would prevent us from carting it away, we said, we would pass the baton to them, and the workers who built this machine never stopped smiling.

Though I was not a general, I created the strategy for defending the city. All the generals professed to be impressed, even those who did not habitually butter up the queen. We built sectional walls throughout the city, just as we had done in the reservoir, and according to exactly the same rationale—to break the momentum and pressure of assaulting waves. And while we were erecting impediments we were also clearing channels and making roads

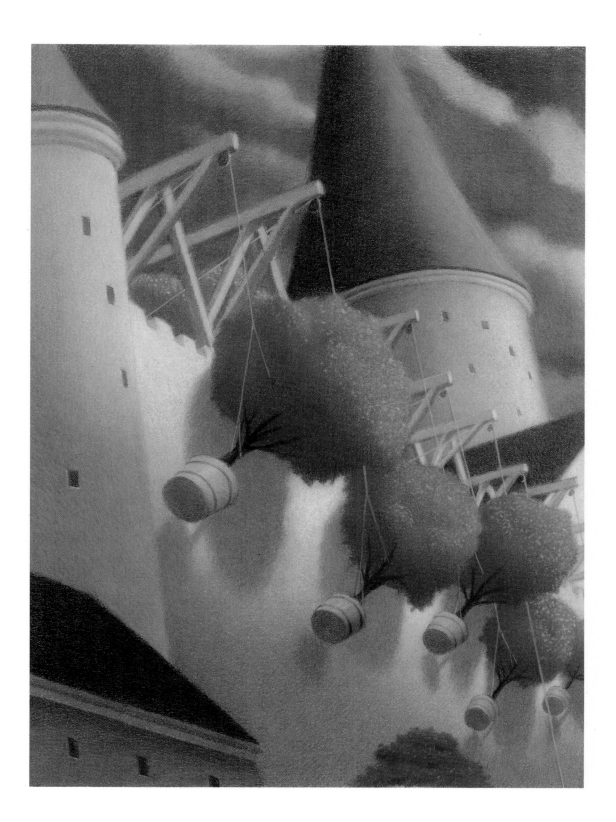

that mercilessly cut through the city but that would amplify the powers of our diminished armies by allowing them to move so fast they could almost be in four places at once. Every sector had teams for reconnaissance, damage control, care of the sick and wounded, householding and supply, communications, etc. And then there were the mobile brigades, cavalry mostly, that would reinforce a weak point with overwhelming strength after galloping along the network of new roads.

That was it. We worked hard, and when it was done it was done, and we waited. In this peculiar twilight time, when so many people forgave and were reconciled to one another, we lived in a holy city that even as we moved toward winter seemed full of quickening light. As much as we could, we retired from affairs of state and things of the world. Families stayed by their fires. Courting couples became inseparable. The old became stiller yet, listening to the clocks that tick even for the young. And the queen remained most of the time in the royal apartments, alone with her son. For hour upon hour she spoke to him, though he could not understand, of chances lost and chances left, of history, hope, and courage, of his father, and of love, although of that she had hardly to say a word.

Autumn started soft and turquoise and then became sapphire and clear. The lake kicked up in white-topped boat-swamping swells; the same wind that gelled the sides of black waves stripped the trees of their orange blaze; and the falling leaves were like Greek fire on paper boats drifting through columns of cold shadow. Winter came early in December, covering the plains with the white that even in summer had never strayed from the mountaintops. The snow was pleasing: we had our house in order, and the usurper's armies would have to camp on fields as hard and cold as ice.

ON THE TWENTY-NINTH OF DECEMBER, A CRUEL and sunless day, a sentry at the southeast corner of the wall reported that the snow seemed to be melting, that the plain seemed to be rolling up toward us like the brown edge that moves along a burning piece of paper. This sudden thaw, we soon discovered, was the effect of the usurper's armies blotting out the snow.

Two million men covered the wintered plain until it looked like a field in May, and on the first evening their hundred thousand fires burned like stars that had stuck and flared in the raw earth. Supply trains never ceased to move in hundreds of gossamer lines disappearing over the horizon. At night their bright torches seemed to jiggle up and down. In the day and from a distance the long lines of horses and camels looked like black spider webs swaying in slow motion on the wind.

Ten thousand siege engines, many larger than our own, were brought close, and long ladders were stacked up like piles of twigs. And they were boiling oil. What for? Because we were on the walls, it was our job to pour boiling oil on them, and this was the cause of much resentment. It led the Tookisheims to claim that the usurper's men were friendly, and were merely making soup, an interpretation that was rejected after they pumped it into high-pressure hoses and squirted it over the walls in lines of flame that looked like dragon pee.

And, with their machines, what did they throw at the walls and into the city? What did they *not* throw? Boulders, of course, and every other kind of rock; bombs; bladders of flaming oil; cannonballs; sharpened chains that whizzed through the air and decapitated steeples; dead animals infected with plague; lead pellets that routinely broke every window in the city; crazed fighting jackals that descending under silken canopies, bit themselves free upon landing, and then fiercely attacked anything with a pulse; and arrows, fleets of them, so that all our wooden buildings looked like porcupines in heat.

We ourselves worked hard showering the enemy with projectiles and flames, and after a month or two it began to feel like the ordinary state of things. As the usurper's ships prowled the lake, we turned to the reservoir, which, because of all the churning, did not freeze. We were optimistic of survival, though we realized that our opponents had not made their first charge, had not broken into the city, and had yet to breach the wall.

The first attempt came on a frozen night in February. We watched as two million soldiers dressed for battle. These were our own people, fighting sadly against us, but ferociously, and when the first blow came the city almost collapsed upon itself.

From a crescent of ten thousand archers, arrows would flow in a continuous stream toward one narrow point, at which the siege engines and ten to twenty towers would slowly move. Nothing could be done, no oil poured, no arrows or shot rained down upon them, because of the covering fire that made it impossible even to peek over the battlements. In this way, they breached the wall in fifty places, positioning ten or twenty stair towers, and a hundred flimsy ladders in between. In a few minutes, a thousand men would pour into a single breach, so that within the space of half an hour, they had fifty thousand men within the walls, with hundreds of thousands lined up behind them ready to follow.

We channeled each penetration by keeping strong pressure on it from left and right, and that day three hundred thousand enemy soldiers were forced into terrible battles in the narrow streets.

Though it was my own plan, I shuddered to think of its effect. Five thousand of the usurper's soldiers, screaming havoc and death, would charge down a street only wide enough for two wagons. When they had surged as far as their numbers could support, and had begun to slow with doubt, we lowered a gate in front of them. Now they were in a tight pen, trapped between the gate before them and the battlements behind.

By the thousand—for we, too, had armies—our archers appeared in the windows and on the rooftops. The arrows flew so thickly in both directions, with hundreds colliding head on and many splitting in two, that the air looked like the sunlight space above a wild threshing floor. And when it was done, God forgive us, the only way to clear the streets of the dead was to hurl them over the wall.

We held that day and in the days after, but we lost so many soldiers and our hearts became so heavy that we began to picture defeat. Time passed very painfully. After six surges, the decimation of the armies, and the loss of half the city, we were still in winter, and it was still deadeningly cold and dark. Even the streets that were ours were unsafe: raiding parties emerged from the sewers, from over the rooftops, and from the neck of the catapults, to descend noiselessly by silken parachute. As we died slowly by degree, defeat began to rise like the sun.

Everything was in short supply—wood for fires, medicine and food, heat, arms and ammunition, human energy, and hope. By every measure, as we became weaker, the enemy grew stronger, until we began to wonder if perhaps we deserved our fate, if God had ceased to favor us and now looked kindly upon our foe.

By mid-March, as the sun grew stronger over land still covered in snow, we had lost two-thirds of the city, including the reservoir. The loyal, the faithful, and those who were barely alive had taken refuge in the palace. Now under the usurper's law, the city took to life in the regimented fashion of the previous regime. The markets were active once again. The streetcars ran. Soldiers in neat ranks rode silently on the Ferris wheels.

Sometime in March—I don't remember when, for I was too tired to make sense of time—we heard a great roar from without the palace walls. We thought this was the cheer before the final assault, for they had been so thoroughly marshalling their forces and building so many engines and towers that they would have to come at us only one time. It was to have been an overwhelming blow, and the more their preparations continued within our sight, the harder it was for us to maintain our flagging will to fight.

But it was not the cheer before an assault, it was a shout of victory. Bulgatia had fallen, Astrahn was dead, the armies in chains. We, then, were the only ones left. Against the usurper's reinforced and replenished armies we could throw just a hundred thousand men, half of whom were sick and the other half dizzy with hunger.

And yet the queen would not surrender. She was not born to surrender, and for that we loved her, though we were certain we were about to fall. She was splendid then, even if her mind sometimes wandered, even if she sometimes seemed distracted, and even if she spoke to her child of his father as if the father still lived. Perhaps this was the price she paid for being resolute in the face of the enemy. "Defy them," she said to her trembling army, weak even from lack of water. "Defy them. For now that we have nothing, defiance is all."

IN EARLY SPRING COME THE WINDS THAT SIGNAL THE breakup of the ice. And though the surface of the lake remains as solid as if it will last forever, the snow blows across it in cold lines of blue that mimic ice fractured in the sun. From the city the armies of air passing over the lake seemed both mysterious and terrible. What animates such frigid air? What gives it power and velocity? And to what battle is it directed with such apparent resolve that it makes of drifts of snow nothing more than stunned arrows pointing to where it has disappeared?

When all but the queen were reconciled to die, when we felt as if we knew the wind and where it was going, and were no longer afraid to think of going with it, the Duke of Tookisheim's purple carriage rolled up to the palace gates and waited for permission to enter, which, after a time, was granted.

As they made their way toward the royal apartments, he and his retainers looked out of their gilt-framed windows of deep gray glass and saw the faces of our soldiers. Not the soundproofing of his carriage but the absolute silence of our men rattled the Duke of Tookisheim, who could not believe that, because he himself would not, anyone else could fight beyond all calculation, all advantage, and all prospect of victory. We fought not for victory or advantage, but because the fighting as we lasted became a song that we did not want to stop singing, and it was that song itself that gave us life. No wonder the Duke of Tookisheim could not understand. All he and his kind could do was calculate, something at which we, alas, had proved not too skilled.

We led him into the queen's presence, and this was a sight to see, our almost emaciated sovereign who would eat only the rations of a common soldier, and the Duke of Tookisheim, swollen like a hog's bladder floating down a stream in the hot sun. She, delicate and thin, her lovely chestnut hair floating about skin as smooth as ivory, and he, florid, pitted, and bewigged. She, with thin tortoise-shell spectacles, smelling of roses, voice chastened by defeat. He, in spectacles of snake-colored metal with sequined scales, smelling of octopus and marmalade (his breakfast), voice like a calliope and beating drum. She, a hundred and twenty pounds. He, two hundred and seventy. She, with eyes in which floated worlds. He, with the eyes of a fish late to market.

"What is it, Tookisheim?" she asked, abandoning formalities.

"Majesty!" he answered, with the sarcasm of a cat who is polite to a mouse. "Have you had enough to eat?"

"Not by your standards," she replied.

"I beg your pardon?"

"Not if one measures lunch in octopuses."

"Octopuses, Majesty, or, as the scholars might say, octo-*pies*, are a breakfast food."

"Whole?" asked the queen.

The Duke of Tookisheim's face became almost angelic as he said, "When stuffed with marmalade, asparagus, and lemon chiffon."

"Thank you for making me happy that I have hardly eaten in the last six months. I would not have thought it would be possible."

"Delighted," he said, bowing slightly, fake birthmark twitching.

"Well? What do you want? You have moved from the place where you were to the place where you are. You don't do that except if you want something."

"Would you care to surrender?" he asked. "No one will be executed except you and your child. The others will be spared, I think."

At first we were as stunned as if a bomb had just exploded and we had been visited with the customary paralysis. But then we unfroze.

"No!" shouted a soldier who would not otherwise have dared speak to his queen. She forgave him, it seemed, perhaps because she herself had not known what to say. Had the price been her death alone, she would immediately have accepted it. But not even to save hundreds of thousands of her subjects would a woman see her child murdered. It simply is not written that way, and never will be.

And our queen, whose heart went out to the fathers and sons who manned her armies, all of them mothers' children, was broken by this, and remained speechless. I joined in the insubordination, I too said "no," and the same word soon followed with absolute conviction from every man in the room. The queen looked at Tookisheim, as if in amazement, and said, "My husband, when he returns from the Veil of Snows, will thrash you." In that moment, I wanted desperately to embrace her, and in that moment some of the soldiers bent their heads in pity.

Then two sergeants grabbed Tookisheim and dragged him out, bumping his bulk down the steps and throwing him back into his purple carriage, which bounced so hard on its springs that the retainers were thrown against the frescoed ceiling and the jingling of their necklaces and jewels sounded like a box of sleigh bells thrown down the stairs of a steeple.

That was when the queen laughed at first, and then, pivoting toward me, cried for all the terrible things to come. And that was when I took her into my arms, for although I was only a soldier, and women hesitated even to look upon me, and she was my sovereign, there was no one else. Perhaps nothing is as strong or fine as unrequited love when by discipline it is kept properly in its place, but I'm glad that, for this short time, I held her, as delicately as ever I could, for it had been so long since anyone had, and it was the last time that anyone would.

THOSE OF US WHO REMAINED SEEMED TO REALIZE simultaneously that for standing fast in the palace itself we would be hunted through the darkness of its lowest labyrinths, and we could not see ourselves, much less our lovely queen, hiding in bins of rotted feed with the rats, or emerging with whitened eyes from the dust of coal chutes to engage small detachments of the usurper's armies in increasingly futile engagements.

"We can't escape across the lake," the queen said to her generals, "as we don't have enough boats, and even if we did they would be sunk, for we long ago gave up the navy, thinking that we didn't need a navy on a lake that was entirely our own. And if we had the boats and if we had a navy, and reached the other side, where would we go? The only direction in which to flee would take us to Bulgatia."

We all knew what she had in mind, and that she wanted us to think of it ourselves, so we did.

"Is there any hope?" she asked. "In what direction can we turn?"

"The mountains, Majesty," said a wizened general from the time of the old emperor, a white-haired ancient with mustaches like clouds. "Only in the mountains do we have a chance."

The queen straightened and her eyes seemed less filled with sadness, for the mountains were where she had spent her girlhood, raised by the royal tutor who she had thought was her grandfather, and where eventually she had learned that she, a simple girl with no pretenses, was the rightful queen. That she had come down to the plain not to avenge her murdered forebears but to keep faith with them was nothing less than the history of us all. And now that she wanted to go back, it seemed right, just right, exactly so, for as you fall you reach for what you love and what you know.

The old general continued. "There," he said, "we will have the limitless space in which to dilute any number of the usurper's pursuing forces until they will have to face us one by one. There, if we can reach it, is a place where our children may find shelter, anonymity, and peace."

"The mountains," said the queen, gravely, for she knew the price.

"If . . ." the general went on, "if we reach them alive, we cannot fail to have left behind at least a half of all who exit the city. The fight to reach the foothills may take ninety of a hundred soldiers, or we may fail to break through. Still, I cannot imagine that a single one of your soldiers, or any of their families, would prefer to die here rather than in the open air."

"We can't poll them," the queen said. "There is no time, and if there were, the spies would give us away."

"When we break out," the general confirmed, "it must be with no more than an hour of preparation. Some will enter the grates and tunnels knowing only then what has been decided."

"If we march out straight," Notorincus said, "they'll attack us from both sides and ahead. Our column will be like a strudel in a room full of rats."

I then remembered my role as strategist. Although I could not claim to have broken the siege, we were still alive, and in war that is a fine credential. "We'll go east," I said, "using the lake to protect our northern flank, and the city the western. Toward the east the enemy's sparse deployments stop five minutes' ride from the battlements. He'll turn everything he has from the plain to attack our southern flank, which, of necessity, will be long. But his armies will choke into slow-moving columns as he tries to reach us, and the effect of their overwhelming numbers will be lessened. Our archers and pikemen will defend the long column of march as best they can, while our cavalry runs parallel to our route, breaking up the attacking fronts on the perpendicular, like a knife cutting bread."

"And then we'll turn," the queen said. "This is, what is left of us, and go south to the mountains. After how many days of fighting will we have broken free enough to change direction?"

"Three or four," the generals said. This was the kind of thing they knew.

"And what are our chances?" the queen asked.

"It is likely," replied the old general, knowing that he himself would never see steep white mountains over dark blue meadows, "that some will get through. A hundred, perhaps, or twenty."

NO MATTER THE SEVERITY OF THE OLD MAN'S estimate, we left the city on the warmest evening of late March, when the enemy had stood his weapons and was three-quarters of the way through a heavy dinner. An hour of sunlight and dusk, and it would be dark.

The eastern flank of the besieging armies had been denuded to bring its best troops into the city for the attack on the palace, and what remained was placed under the command of Straveetz Tookisheim, a rarity in the Tookisheim tribe both because he was a military man and because he did not share the Tookisheim predilections for sloth, filth, indolence, vanity, inanity, and idiocy.

Though a third of their force was comprised of siege engines pointed haplessly toward the battlements, they still outnumbered us five to one in foot soldiers and cavalry, and had great stocks of arrows and shot, which we did not, and they had eaten. In fact, though their recently filled stomachs would slow them in battle, we who were hungry, lithe, and fast envied them for eating even if they were condemned to the Tookisheim diet of fried everything: fried salad, fried apples, fried syrup, fried salt—fried, fried, everything fried—fried water, and fried milk. And all the fried water that they were served at meals was flavored with the batter-fried ink of fried octopuses and squids. What a family, what a clan, what a cuisine.

Our first wave of cavalry burst out of half a dozen secret tunnels spread along the route of escape. From the farthest exit beyond the enemy lines, a thousand horsemen left a fold in the ground and grouped to charge west into the setting sun. At the same time, other thousands appeared, some even from beneath the enemy tents, lifting them like ghosts, and they began to fight along axes of least resistance designed to stun Staveetz's command and split his army into broken sections.

After half an hour of this our five easternmost gates were opened and from each poured two thousand cavalry galloping forth and then reversing direction to create a wall of horsemen behind which the main body could travel along the lakeshore.

At the center of the main body I was with the queen and her personal guard. The infant rode in an upright cradle that hung across the saddle of a strong charger. In his cloths of gold he was then placed in a soft and comfortably padded chamber overhung by a slanting roof of wood and leather. Although he could see out,

neither rain nor missiles could get in, and the frame of the little box was strong enough so that even were the charger to roll on his side it would not be crushed. Carried with him, wrapped, as was he, in golden cloth, were pages written by the queen to tell him of what had come before. She of all people knew that the saddest thing in the world was for a parent to have his child loosed upon the wing, and that of this she stood a good chance. And yet she was unperturbed, for her own parents were as alive in her heart as if she had known them, and perhaps more so.

She was dressed for battle in her customary way, with a light bow, a small sword, and not that many arrows. Though her child was shielded, she wore no armor. It was her duty to be exposed, because her soldiers would be incalculably vigilant and hard-fighting if they knew she was among them, in a rain of arrows, with neither plate nor mail. I, too, wore neither plate nor mail, out of deference to her, and because I could not stand the thought that a shower of crossbow bolts would take her life and leave me unscathed. My sword, however, was a full sword, and my quiver heavy with the strongest arrows. I also held a short lance, the end butted to a cup in my saddle.

For hours we moved forward without the necessity of coun-terattack, so thoroughly had we rattled our opponents, who wast-ed half their strength thrusting through the palace gates, only to find no one inside. We suffered many casualties, though mainly in the cavalry, for the enemy was not alert enough to launch arrows at the scores of thousands who proceeded in back of this shield. Even the old general with the whitened hair was suddenly possessed with new energy as he saw our vast column break out of the enemy cordon days ahead of schedule.

Messengers seeking out our banners arrived in a constant stream, and from one of them we learned of our luck. He arrived just as we were reforming the column to take the blow expected from the south. No one had dared to imagine that the usurper would not wheel his hosts in a semicircle to strike us broadside. But the messenger told us that the usurper had become ill, evidently from something that he had eaten.

Most wonderfully, the Duke of Tookisheim had been given command, an astonishing lapse attributable mainly to the usurper's nausea. Even Peanut must have been shaken to see his father take control of the armies as he did. The duke's purple carriage carried him to a platform on the southwest wall, where he directed the battle with the aid of semaphores and brass telescopes, all the while distracted by a six-hour picnic laid upon linen-covered outdoor tables, many of which would have collapsed from the weight of the champagne bottles standing upon them had he not done his duty in drinking them down to reduce the strain.

The first thing he did, which accounted for our unexpectedly quick passage, was to give a hell-and-thunder speech about crème caramel. His troops, lined up by the hundred thousand, could hardly hear what he was saying, and could hardly see the chef's utensils he brandished like a trial lawyer, but they were only too happy to stay out of the battle. And who but the Duke of Tookisheim could talk with passion, hysteria, and tears about crème caramel for six hours straight, throwing in a homily here and there about the subtleties of fried octopus?

When at last he decided to attack, he had them storm the vacant palace, where he lost half of them in the infinite maze of rooms, halls, and galleries. If I know soldiers, and I do, many a patrol was ended in a featherbed in one of the innumerable apartments, as a hardwood blaze heated what had been drinking water in a shiny nickel apparatus for the bath, and the rich oriental carpets grew ever more lustrous in maturing firelight reflected from cherry paneling.

Completely flummoxed and still gallantly reducing the weight on the suffering picnic tables, the Duke of Tookisheim called for a harpsichord, and when it was brought to him he sat down at it and began to play and sing. This got his blood up, and he shouted out orders to charge. From having witnessed various court entertainments he knew enough of technicalities to get his cavalry going, but most of them he sent either back into the city, stupefied at the walls, or galloping into the lake.

Those ordered to us, randomly, did not wheel from the south but were directed at our rear guard on an extremely narrow front. It was like holding a bridge. Fifty thousand cavalry charged east, but they contacted us only in a line of ten or twenty. The fighting was bitter and their supply of replacements seemingly endless, but they could not even dent our position. This went on through the night, and by midmorning of the next day we found ourselves, still intact, near the foothills.

The queen ordered a counterattack upon the pursuing column, and we wheeled broadside and struck them from two directions at once, breaking them up so decisively that all the forces of what now was the state retreated to regroup. In this lull, ninety thousand of us who were still alive gathered around a windblown knoll to hear the queen speak.

The breeze was soft and the snow melting as she spoke, the great horses in back of her ready to run to new places and graze in unimagined fields. Her voice somehow carried, as it always did, with the wind bringing it as if by magic to every ear. First she looked over the remnants of her kingdom, who stood in unaccountable comfort beneath luffing banners and a pale blue sky.

"Thank God we have been spared. And spared we have

been," she said. "In a moment, my kingdom and yours will cease to exist, for here and now it must come to an end, and from here we will scatter to the mountains to protect our lives. There, ahead, against the Veil of Snows, you will find infinite space for healing, and there, if there is a God, my son will find his father. You will not always be free from the usurper's edicts and impressments. It will all depend upon where you go, how fast you move, and the nature of your luck. All I ask is that you remember. Why, I do not know, except perhaps to love and honor those who are lost, those who, in dying, were robbed of the story ahead—unless my fondest hopes are real.

"Scatter to the far corners of this land, hide on mountainsides and in dells, settle by fast-flowing streams and in the deep sheltering silence of the forest. Scatter, and remember, and perhaps someday our children's children will remember, and faint memories will swell into the fires that will guide them home."

And then, as was her custom, she did not wait to see others do her bidding, but quickly mounted, followed by her guard, who flew into their saddles as if it was not a day of defeat. She cast one last gentle smile back at the silent thousands, took the reins of the charger that carried her son, and spurred her horse.

I do not know what was said or felt as we left, but soon we found ourselves in silence but for the horses' breathing, the sound of hoofbeats, and the creaking of saddlery. We passed streams that had cut through the snow, and flowers that had burst from it, and we made for a faraway crest beyond which seemed to be a world of clouds, a luminous line of red and gold floating above a range of dark hills.

IN THE QUEEN'S GUARD WAS A YOUNG SOLDIER WHO, just as we were breaking free, was badly wounded by the kind of arrow that is launched from a catapult. With a heavy shaft and a blunt head, it is designed for breaking fortifications. Though when he fell he begged the queen to leave him, she would not, and from then on he traveled with us, lying on a frame slung between two yoked-together horses. As this slowed our pace, most of the other mounted detachments disappeared ahead of us into the hills, splaying out in many directions and always pulling away.

After the second day in the foothills we were running and rising in steep forests and over huge plateaux still snow covered but for an occasional newly greening field. The wounded boy could no longer speak. Though we knew he would die we dared not stop, for great armies were following our many tracks, and our only hope was to keep moving either until the strengthening sun obliterated our trail in the snow or we entered regions so remote, so crossed by rivers, so rocky, vast, and steep, that we would simply disappear, inexplicably and in peace.

On the third or perhaps the fourth or fifth night—I cannot remember—we halted on a huge table of rock over which ran shallow streams heated by the sun until the water was hot. And the rock itself, hot and dry, was a welcome change from thawing ground and melted snow.

As soon as we dismounted we started fires and set up kettles of water that, already heated, boiled fast. We tended the dying soldier, took care of the horses, and ate what little we had to eat as the dry wood blazed, the stars came out, and the streams ran in the dark. We were twenty all told, and after we had rested a little we sent out a captain to backtrack and stand guard. If he placed himself well he would hear the approach of horses or see them against even the night sky as they crested a ridge and briefly obliterated bright stars. This was one of the skills of soldiering beyond those of battle. It was floating on the current rather than thrashing against it.

When in early morning the captain returned from his night watch he told us that our track was marked by widely separated spots of blood. Only once every half hour or so, he said, but as regular as a stitch. The blood had come from the wounded boy, whose strength, we hoped, might still carry him through, although our judgment was that it would not.

"What does it matter?" the queen asked. "We always leave the compacted tracks of twenty horses, indelible upon rock, lasting for weeks in soft earth and for days or more in snow."

"The tiny drops of blood, Majesty," replied the captain, "probably stretch all the way to the knoll, where we left many of our banners, and where, with only slight consideration, the enemy would place your speech to our army before it scattered. The hoofprints of our horses would have been lost amid the hundreds of thousands that chopped the snow in that place as the army broke up and followed us. But any good tracker should be able to disentangle our path from all the others by following the scarlet trace. We are not safe."

"And when will we be safe?" the queen asked.

"Only when he stops bleeding or is left behind."

"We don't leave our wounded behind," the queen said, "even if they are heroes who beg for it."

"Even if it may lead to the death of your child?"

The queen lifted her head almost like an animal catching a scent, and she said, "Yes, even if it may lead to that."

"It means that we must ride slowly," the captain told her, eyes cast down, "while our pursuers ride fast."

These were hardly easy times for the queen, but she only grew in her graces. "You have observed deer, Captain, have you not? You have even hunted them?"

"Yes, Majesty."

"So have I observed them. They are born to be hunted and pursued, and they are born defenseless. I watched in the forest when I was a girl, and then, later, after I had become queen, and my nobles hunted them. All they can do is run, and they do, but many of them are taken. How is it, do you suppose, that they can live, knowing this, knowing that at any time their children can be cut down, or they themselves, leaving children alone in the world? How is it, Captain, that, knowing this, they can live?"

"I don't know, Majesty. I only hunted them. I did not put myself in their place."

"Now you are in their place."

"Yes."

"And now you must do as they do."

"Be nervous, Majesty?"

She laughed. "No, not nervous, but alert. And grateful. Let all sensation thunder in, stay with those you love, and trust in the time you have left."

And then, knowing that our time was marked, we mounted and rode on, lifted by love and defiance, listening to all sound, galloping toward mountains and light.

IN THE HIGH COUNTRY OF THIS KINGDOM THE LIGHT deepens, confuses, and protects. Mountainsides that from a distance might look flat are ennobled by light and shadow that give them dark and precipitous clefts and roll the summits like windblown clouds. The light will vary in such a way that valleys once colliding will seem to run apart, and vast calderas, like patches upon the ocean, drift from places thought fixed.

I do not know how many days we rode, or weeks or months, for it was easy to lose track of time in the light and lovely colors, and in the hundred miles of deep blue. We hardly spoke as we moved through forests somnolent in eternal peace, past sparkling lakes enclosed by rings of purple granite. The insistent motion of our horses driving ever deeper into God's country was a steadily building song that we dared not interrupt. We would stop at dusk, and after eating and washing would fall into the kind of sleep that knits together the strengths of the next day. And then we were off before sunrise, rising hour by hour into the increasingly sharp air.

The boy did not die until early one afternoon when we stopped by the shallows of a cold river that shone in the sun. The last thing he knew was the clean smell of waters newly born from ice, and then he left us. We used the water boiling above our fires to prepare him for burial, and set about digging a grave in the chalky soil under a little bluff where we had taken shelter from the wind.

As the sun reflected almost blindingly from the river and the rock it was warm there, and I was resting, when the queen approached me. I began to stand so that I could sink to one knee, but she signaled me to stay. She sat on a boulder behind me and to the right, where, if I were looking straight ahead, I could not see her. The baby was sleeping in its cradle on the horse, which grazed on wet grass that came up between the river-polished rocks. With eighteen soldiers left, the kingdom that once had been ours seemed only like a dream.

"Now they won't even have a trail of blood to follow," she said, with regret. "Do you think they're close?"

"I don't know," I replied over the sound of the waters, "but they would have had no infant to spare on hard roads, no wounded man, and, forgive me, your grace, no queen for whom one's regard leads to what might have been fatal courtesy."

She was astonished. "I thought we were riding as hard as we could."

"Oh no ma'am," I said, my deep love for her contained within me by sad and perfect discipline. "Had we left the boy behind, we could have ridden much harder, much faster, and used up more of the nights. We might have worn out some horses, but we would have gone twice as far. We would never, my dear lady, have stopped for a midday meal."

"We must ride like that now," she said, "until we go so deeply into these mountains that we can never be found."

"They're following the trail now, Majesty, not the blood, but we'll move faster."

"I'll feed the baby as I ride. I've done it already."

"Yes."

"I want to drive so deep that when finally we stop we'll have no idea of what is real."

I nodded, thinking of what had once been unthinkable, of passing the rest of my life with this young queen, and watching her age, while living at the edge of a glacier and by a full speeding stream, of becoming the old man who would instruct the young prince in what he lost and how to retrieve it, of pipes and flutes that echoed in the farthest valleys, of years of fires sweet and hot in darkness crowned by the ice of stars.

"But shall we not leave now?" she asked, for there was something about that bluff, where the stream took a slight turn onto a high plain at the foot of mountains that we guessed to be the highest of any that were. Beyond them, we thought, were lower and gentler lands more remote than any we had ever dreamed of.

"We'll ride as soon as the boy is buried. Those mountains may be the last and highest range."

"I want to see the forests that no one has ever seen," she said. "I want my son to grow up where the green is infinite and there is no time."

"Time will mean nothing to him."

"And he will remember nothing of the city that was," she said.

"Ma'am, when I was young I lived with my mother and father in a house near the march-lands. It was modest but beautiful, and as a child I imagined that it would always last."

"Has it?"

"I don't know. I've never been back, but when I first came to the capital, in the time of your grandfather, I worked at building houses and discovered something sad and true. I learned that houses are delicate frames that hold people only tenuously, that walls and floors are made of weak pieces weakly stitched together, that they are broken apart by rain and snow, by gravity, and the movement of the earth. I learned that they go quickly in fire, and that windows shatter in a storm and doors are broken by enemies and those who are angry. I learned that there is no safety and no shelter in anything we can build or do, that the safest and most sheltering place is in the open, in what we call forever."

She understood, and I saw that she was content. I take comfort in that, for those moments, under the open sky by the river, were her last.

SOMETHING TOLD ME THAT ALL WAS NOT RIGHT. I turned to the grave, where the men were gathered, and counted them. They were seventeen, I was with the queen, our horses were hobbled and grazing. Out of sorrow for the boy, the sentries had come down from the bluff, and no one was watching or in the rearguard.

I stood to order them back, but before the words could leave me I heard a whistle almost like the cry of a marmot, and an arrow pierced my left shoulder from behind. When things such as this happen so much occurs at once and so quickly that time turns from water dashing across rocks to honey that will not leave the jar.

Our soldiers went for their weapons and horses, for they had turned as I stood and their eyes had been upon me as I was struck. A hundred helmets and the tips of bows bloomed from the top of the bluff that had hidden the enemy's approach, and he came from behind us as well from the side, and detachments of riders suddenly appeared across the stream.

The queen had dropped to the ground and was about to rush for her son when I told her to pull out the arrow. I would not be able to fight otherwise. In one leap she moved behind me, but then as she pulled all she did was pull me toward her. "I can't get it," she said.

"Put your foot on my back."

She did, and pulled, and as the arrow came out I fell face forward onto the rocky ground. I felt a terrible pain where the arrow had been, but I forgot my pain when I saw the queen racing to the charger through air that had become wood-colored with arrows. The archers fired fast and mechanically from all around, and as I stood I was struck by another arrow. It opened a wound in my thigh and pushed on to kill a man behind me. I knelt and drew my bow. Never had I been so concentrated, and my targets were obligingly lined up in a row. Though their arrows crisscrossed in the air, they stayed clear of me, and I knocked at least ten archers from the chalky cliff.

Half our men were already dead when the attacking cavalry rode in, swords flashing, horses breathing hard. As I dropped my bow and drew my sword I saw that the queen had mounted and was riding at full gallop toward her son. She cut the line that held his charger, brought her sword back, and struck the horse hard on the withers with the flat so that he would run, anywhere, to save the child.

Then Notorincus and another man appeared, mounted, leading my horse. They stopped only briefly, and I flew into the saddle, spurring the horse the moment I was on his back. Enemy cavalry was converging on the queen, and the charger with her infant son had been forced into the stream, where the water was up to the belly of the war horse and he went rampant to strike infantrymen who tried to kill him with pikes and swords, but who, in steady rhythm, were swept off their feet and into the current either as he struck them down or as they lost their footing on the slick rock. The river now was white and red. Blood filled the water, in pools that quickly stretched into lines as thin as ropes and thread.

As I galloped to the queen, who was on her horse, fighting in the shallows, wielding her sword against foot soldiers and cavalry, the man to my left was knocked from his saddle by an arrow. He went over the neck of the horse and died before he hit the ground, while Notorincus and I, who reached the queen, at least had the satisfaction of being mounted, armed, and at the side of our sovereign as she fought.

As her sword battered their pewter-colored armor and chain—the officers, in the color of black, had held back—she kept an eye on the charger as he was driven farther into the deepening stream. The wooden cradle repeatedly flew into the air and banged against the saddle. Half the time it was suspended in blue and the other half it was slamming against the dark leather over the dappled gray coat. As his mother fought fiercely to get to him and the baby cried, more and more men surrounded her. Even as she struck them down one after another and we cut them into pieces as if they had been apples, they crowded the river until you could hardly see the water.

A thousand men or more had been sent after us, and had persevered. Twenty men cannot fight a thousand. Two men and a woman cannot fight a thousand, even if she is a queen, and even if they love her.

I glanced at Notorincus, and before I turned away I saw him lifted from his horse by a pike. Poor Notorincus, after a flight through the air, fell and disappeared into the mass of dull armor. I turned to the queen. "Notorincus is gone," I said.

She answered silently, moving her lips. I never knew what she said. And we fought on. God knows we fought on, until the charger slipped on its side and went into the water, cradle underneath, and we could fight no longer.

The queen spurred her horse toward her son's, which, thrashing, was beginning to float downstream, but we could not move forward through the mass of men surrounding us. The queen lifted her sword and threw it at a soldier who had gripped her horse's bridle, killing him, but another jumped to his place.

Now she had no sword, now she had no arrows, someone reached up and pulled off her spectacles, and the charger was floating full in the stream. As I cut down soldier after soldier, and tried to make a channel through their ranks, she stood on the back of her horse and leapt toward the water. She landed amid a group of amazed and flattened enemy, who fell back in a ring to give her space.

I did what she had done, but as I flew toward her I was struck many times with sword and stave, and I landed at her feet, bloody and hardly able to move. We could no longer even see the deep part of the stream, and as the young queen knelt in shallow water, she put her hand on the small of my back.

"I'm sorry," she said, and she wept.

The only thing I could say, as I coughed blood, was no, no, and no again, and I kept saying no as I tried to struggle to my feet. Then an officer appeared, a young man, who ordered his men to step back to clear a view of the river.

Far down the stream we saw what looked like a round white

rock moving through the rapids, drawn away from us so quickly that at first it was a spot and then it was only the memory of a spot, and then all we could see was a line of something that looked like white wool, the surface of distant roiling water.

"That was your son," the officer said to the queen, who now wanted only to die. "The story ends here."

I was lying in the bloody water, facing her, when I saw her bow her head to pray. Words would not come from me. I had to move. I knew I could not fight, but I had nothing else to do but try. And then I saw a huge sword rise in the air behind her.

OUR LIVES ARE NOT WHAT WE THINK. THEY ARE CUT down not at our will, and extended not at our will, as was mine, thank God, though at the time this was not what I had wanted, not after what I had seen.

When they killed her, they forgot about me. Their struggle had ended in victory, their campaign was over. With brutality that verged on madness, they threw us into the current. The queen was dead. The river took her quickly, and I hope mercifully, in that it was infinitely long, cold, and pure. I wished then that I would follow, but the river would not oblige.

Though it took her sadly and forever, it merely closed my

wounds and stopped my bleeding. It roused me enough so that I knew to keep my head above water as I was carried downstream. It threw me against rocks, shocking me awake and into life. And soon I was floating at great speed through white water that I assumed would be the last thing I would know. The site of the battle was left behind so quickly and easily, with not a soldier or a horse to be seen, that I questioned memory and doubted my sanity as I choked on water, air, and sun.

Even infinite rivers need not be entirely straight, and this one took its turns where it wanted, wheeling left and right as it cut through cliffs or slowed to swirl around sparkling sandbars and in darkening pools. I was so cold that I could no longer feel my body and was pulled toward sleep, which is, I suppose, how one comes to terms with drowning slowly in a cold stream.

And then the river led me around a bend, the water slowed and warmed, and I was pushed into a deep still pool, where for days or weeks sun-heated water had risen to the surface and now was as hot as a bath. Here I stayed, slowly twirling, until I crawled out onto a bank of dry white sand. I slept and dreamt, and when I awoke I tried to stand. I pulled one leg toward my chest, then painfully pushed forward with my arms until I had one knee on the ground and my thigh upright. The other leg quickly followed suit, and I straightened myself. On my knees I was now high

enough to see some distance down the sandbar, and after a few seconds I realized that not too far from me were tracks that started from the water's edge.

When finally I stood, shakily, I saw that they were hoofprints, and that the horse had been shod. What if, I thought . . . what if the charger had turned over in the stream (after all, we might not have seen it) soon enough so that the baby had not drowned? Probably not, I thought. "Very unlikely," I said out loud even as I began to follow the tracks as fast as I could move. I knew from my own peculiar history that once I had begun something I rarely gave up, and I envisioned myself chasing a horse (which can, after all, find sustenance in grass) across an endless region of plains, forests, and mountains. Have you ever chased a horse even across a meadow?

Still, as I tried to weigh the sense of what I was doing I found myself doing it without cease, and never was there any possibility that I would break off. If the child had lived, he had to be saved. I owed his mother my life and more in the attempt, as I would any mother of any child. And if he had lived not only would I have a son and the queen smile in heaven, but the life of the kingdom would be saved.

The ground beyond the riverbed was hard and sometimes rocky, the trail difficult to follow, but I followed it even in moonlight, past moonlight into starlight, and past starlight to the dawn. I was hungry, aching, cold, and lame, and had no idea where I was going except up. The horse was interested in only one thing. He was a riser. He sought altitude.

Soon I too was rising, through steep forests, meadows, and onto snow-covered plateaux over which I could see the tracks in all light. I might even have been able to find them and follow had the stars been obliterated by cloud. The horse took every upward turn and made any choice to ascend. I found the climb exhausting and overpowering. A child may need me, I told myself, and not just a child, but the child of a woman that I deeply love still. And not just the child of the woman that I deeply love, but the king, into whose service I am sworn and to whom I owe even more than my life.

NOW AND THEN I HAD TO SLEEP, ALTHOUGH I TRIED not to, hoping to steal a march on the horse as he rested at night. I feared for the child, as the higher we went the colder it got, and he was carried across the snow with neither food nor water nor a heavy coverlet. After I had slept for a few minutes, I would force myself to go on, and this way I began to gain on the charger, whose tracks were looking so fresh that had I only been unwounded enough to run I could have caught him in an hour.

And then after tracking them across a night of stars I saw them ahead of me in the rose light of dawn, drawing away on a vast mountain snowfield that was a world in itself. Rivers that the morning sun made red came hurtling from walls of granite the color of charcoal and silver. They floated through the air, braiding and untangling ribbons of white spray, slowly, politely, and without a sound. They came from so far up it was impossible to see where they started, and when they reached the foot of the cliffs they cut deep channels in the snow and ice and ran violently down the mountainside to water the world. This was the Veil of Snows.

For the first time in my life I saw the white wall, a mountain of light that looks like clean snow frothed in a punishing wind. It moves unpredictably to and fro, sometimes settling, sometimes receding, sometimes racing forward, and it roars. But even if you cannot hear yourself speak when you are half an hour's walk from the base, when you are close to it speech is the last thing on your mind.

The horse halted by a crescent in one of the rivers and stood calmly in the sunshine. He could not have been more than six of his own lengths from the wall, and fearing that it would come forward to swallow him up I began to run even though the running

111

opened my wounds and overburdened my heart. In the bright light I had difficulty seeing, but I could make out the cradle, upright and sound, resting against the charger's side. As I got closer I saw a little arm suddenly thrust out from the cradle window beneath the overhang. I smiled. The little arm moved in the raw way that babies move, with quick and dictatorial energy. He was alive! All I had to do was get to him, take the bridle of the charger, and lead them down the mountain.

For fear of spooking the horse, I began to walk. Although I was cold and worn and my heart thundered in my chest, I walked slowly and confidently, trying to stay the horse from movement by imagining how I would seize the bridle. As I neared the horse I heard the baby's cry carried over the falling water.

I was close, almost there, and could see that this horse was in place until led away. Many different joys began to arise at once, but then, from out of the wall, in an instant, came a hundred bowmen and cavalry riding a hundred blood-colored horse of the Golden Horde. They were as dark as mahogany, and their eyes seemed unable to see this world. They looked past me, seeming to know exactly what they had come to do.

I was running and shouting, to no avail, and as I ran toward them I saw two women dismount and approach the cradle. They were smiling, and whereas I was moving as slowly as in a dream

they were moving faster than I could believe. One lifted the overhang and the other took hold of the child. She raised him briefly above her toward the sun, and kissed him.

I was almost there, but I was caught in amber. They put him down on the snow, washed him in a matter of seconds, and wrapped him in a cloth redder than anything in nature. Although I desperately did not want them to take him, what they did seemed right and natural, and I was running as if in slow motion, crying out to people who seemed neither to see nor hear me, deafened by thunder, asking that it not be a dream.

The first woman mounted her horse and was given the baby. She strapped him to her front as the second woman went back to the cradle and took from it the queen's book wrapped in gold cloth. As they began to move back whence they had come, a man at the end of the line appeared to notice me. He drew his short bow and put an arrow in it. As his horse walked him half disappearing into the wall, he aimed the arrow at me.

Clearly these people, with their sturdy and shaggy horses, their homes high in the ice world and close to the sun, their silent demeanor, and their otherworldly eyes, could have shot an arrow halfway around the world and hit whatever it was they were aiming for. I stopped, thinking that I was going to die, and as I watched the child recede, the threatening bowman simply stepped out of our time and into another. They were gone, and only the roar of the water and wall were left.

I approached the white front, which disappeared straight up as far as I could see, and as it seemed to be stable, oscillating only slightly as if in a technique for holding its place, I touched it with my finger. I felt nothing, and thrust in my arm, and then I realized that when the arm was inside it was gone, as if it had been dissolved a million years before, or had never existed. Inside, everything became even, all was nothing, and nothing was all. I could not imagine stepping in, perhaps to stay forever, or perhaps to find myself, washed clean, standing once again in this world.

How was it that the Golden Horde could enter and re-enter seemingly at will? And where was the child? Where was my queen? As these questions were too great for me, and still are, I stepped away. As I walked backward from the roar I tried to tell myself that it was all a dream. But then, after I turned, I saw the charger and the cradle, I touched them, I knew that it was real, and I began to lead the horse down the mountain. I did not enter the white fume, though someday, of course, I will, for I was the only one who knew the tale, and my duty, therefore, was to remain.

✦   ✦   ✦

AND SO I HAVE BEEN HERE FOR TWENTY-FIVE YEARS, and though I have lost faith so often I cannot count the times, I have not lost faith at all, for in the bright of morning, just as I arise, I find my faith restored.

It is now against the law to say the name of the queen or her son, or even to hint at who they were. In all this time, you might think, I would have ceased to recall the surprising particulars, the warm smiles, the faces that eventually one cannot see anymore in photographs, as their stillness camouflages them against the passage of time and petrifies them in memory.

But I have not forgotten, for I believe in the unfolding of the tale, that, like water, it cannot be suppressed in its simple will to rise, if it is fed by rains and comes in abundance. The only thing that lasts is the unfolding of the tale, the only thing of which you can be sure.

Devotion becomes waiting, and waiting becomes devotion, and as I waited I became more certain, even though all logic conspired against it. And then this morning the bucket was blasted away on the stream. I have always drawn water from that bucket, and I had no other way of bringing water back to my room.

I walked slowly up the hill, and when I returned home I went out on my little mountaineer's balcony and watched the clear light from the east as it warmed the Veil of Snows. Then I began to write this tale. I could hardly keep up with it as it flooded from pen to page, perhaps because it had been waiting so long to be told, or perhaps because its only form was the simple truth.

For many hours under the bright sun I worked desperately hard and in the deepest concentration. I neither ate nor drank nor even moved, and time passed with such great speed that I seemed to finish only a moment after I had begun. Weak with hunger, exhaustion, and thirst, I fell asleep, and was awakened only when the sun crossed over the roof and left me in cool shadow. I was so hot I could barely get up, and I had to have water.

I went for the bucket automatically, but it was not there. Half awake and hardly able to walk, I felt that I was dreaming the end of things, or at least the end of me. Nothing seemed solid or true. I knew I could not walk down to the river again. I knew that I had never been as old or as weak, and that I had to have water.

In twenty-five years I hadn't touched the blue bottle. The water within was the past itself, and I had always promised that I would save it until the kingdom was restored. But I broke my promise, and dizzy and disoriented I abandoned my discipline and seized the bottle by its cobalt blue neck and took it out onto the balcony, where remnants of the morning heat radiated luxuriously from the wood.

Well, I thought, better that I drink it than some stranger after I'm gone. This was just a rationale for my weakness, but I was moved by something more than thirst. Though I was merely opening a bottle of water, I felt that I had betrayed all that I had believed in. I looked at it, amazed, as it bubbled after so long on the shelf and the light came perfectly through the blue. I smelled it, and it seemed to be fresher even than whitewater from the river.

This was the water of the old kingdom, and I drank it down. It was as good as on the day it had been bottled, and I came alive with regret, for I had not only lost faith, I had acted upon loss of faith, and now nothing was left.

So I threw the bottle high into the air, and it spun neck over base as it descended to the rocks and the river below, turning the water briefly into a shower of glistening blue as it shattered, its sinking shards to be carried down to the plain, or perhaps just to settle in a cold black pool hidden somewhere within the trees.

Though I looked out at the Veil of Snows, prepared for deep sadness, what I saw was like an electric current that snapped through my body and danced in front of my eyes. Half the snow-fields had turned as dark as mahogany, and the dark consumed the light as the Golden Horde marched down the mountainsides in a host larger than I had ever imagined, having switched allegiances, and come to our side, or so I prayed.

And, yes, it was so. In the lead of this army, as if tugging a shadow, were two immense columns that from a distance looked like braided threads. They were horsemen and soldiers in the colors red, of the father, and gold of the son, and though I had to look twice, and three times, and more, to tell myself that it was true, it was true, and I knew, and I would have known even had I not looked at all.

All this time, father and son had been in a place that I could not see, a place where I could not go, a place that I dared not imagine or wish for, in that it is the deepest desire of the human heart, and as we grow old we are taught not to wish for what we want. But in these years they had been together. And although I did not see her, I hoped that the queen, too, was hidden somewhere in the distant color of the march, though that may have been too much even to pray for.

For a moment they were obscured by the shadow of a cloud, and I thought that perhaps I was just an old man dreaming. But then the shadow lifted and I saw that the columns were close and real. And then I saw them, father and son, on the snowfields bright and near, riding together, as once they had done, in a kingdom far and clear.